Lizardville - The Ghost Story

Steve Altier

To Linda
Wishing you a
wonderful day.
Enjoy the book.

Steve Altier

Copyright © 2016 by Steve Altier

Imprint: Dark Cloud Books

Cover photography: Picture of "1904" Ax Factory in Mill Hall. Pennsylvania Historical Society.

ISBN-13:   978-1535309455

ISBN-10:   1535309458

Library of Congress Control Number: 2016913082
CreateSpace Independent Publishing Platform, North Charleston, SC

Printed in the United States of America.

To my wife Toni, who opened my heart and my eyes.

Chapter One

The world outside sounded menacing as loud thunderous cracks rained down on the home. Bright lights filled the night sky, and the gaps in the curtains allowed the lights to race across the room, giving the illusion of figures dancing on the walls. Another flash that sounded like the cracking of a whip was followed by thunder. The sound resonated and vibrated throughout the home. I watched my boys lunge from their chairs, running from window to window like a well-choreographed dance routine, trying to catch a glimpse of the outside world as the lightning display continued.

The wind howled and whistled as it raced past the house. I knew Zack and Daniel had never experienced a storm like this in their lives. More thunder and another lightning strike, this one too close for comfort. The loud pop sent my boys spiraling back from the window. I peeked over my book and watched them bounce into the family room where I was sitting. My youngest, thirteen-year-old Daniel, stayed close behind his older brother as he tried to hide his fear.

The room was large, quiet, and dimly lit by a single reading light that stood behind my old reclining chair. On one of the walls, picture frames reminisced of family memories, a mixture of old and new. Mounted on the north wall was a flat screen television. My chair and a couch sat facing that direction. The tall floor light behind me flickered for a moment as another bolt of lightning rocked the windows. Heavy curtains hid the large bay window on the exterior wall. Faint glowing lights

1

peeked through with each lightning flash. Large oak bookcases flanked the windows, each shelf filled with books.

The wind roared louder, giving the illusion of a freight train passing by our house. As the storm grew in intensity, Zack and Daniel nervously looked at one another and then began to stare at me, watching as I calmly sat in my chair reading one of my many books.

The howling winds grew louder and louder, and the rain pounded on the windows as another bright flash illuminated the room. Another loud crack and the boys jumped once again. The lights flickered for a moment before going out, drowning the room in total darkness.

I, John Malone, was always prepared, as I pulled a box of matches from my front pocket. I opened them, grabbed a match, and struck it against the side of the box. We could hear the sound of the match sliding against the rough sandpaper surface. The smell of sulfur filled my nose as the match ignited into a bright yellow flame.

The light was enough to cast a soft, dim glow across the room. Reaching for the drawer located on the wooden table that sat next to my chair, I opened it, pulled out a short, stubby candle, and placed the match to the candlewick. The smell of the burnt match hung in the air as I shook my hand from side to side to extinguish its flame. I gently tilted the candle to its side, dripping a few drops of hot wax on a small plate that sat on the table next to me. Then I slowly pushed the candle into the liquid puddle, securing it to the plate.

"Zack, Daniel, come over here." I smiled as I motioned them over. "Each of you needs to take a candle," I told the boys and pulled two more from the drawer.

Zack and Daniel seemed a little skittish in the dark; I watched as they made their way toward me. I could see the nervousness in their eyes as they each reached out to take a candle from my hand. Another intense lightning strike hit directly outside the home. Daniel jumped at the blast; I could tell his heart was racing by the look in his eyes. He glanced at his older brother, making sure he hadn't noticed. The lightning had also caught Zack off guard; he flinched as well, and his eyes grew wide. They both gazed at each other and then shared a brief chuckle. I smiled as I watched my two alpha boys trying to hide their fear.

One at a time, Zack and Daniel extended their candles over the flame. The boys glided back to the couch, then plopped themselves down, and cast a glance back to me. Shaking my head from side to side, I stood and grabbed my plate with one hand. I cupped my other hand around the candle flame, forming a barrier to block the breeze as I walked. I could feel the warmth of the candle against my fingers as I tried to ensure my candle stayed lit. The boys seemed impressed. I made my way to the kitchen where I pulled two more small plates from the cupboard and slid them under my plate before returning to the family room.

"Boys, are you going to hold them in your hands until the wax burns your fingers?" I chuckled a bit. Handing one plate to each of the boys, I showed them how to secure the candle to the plate with a few drops of hot wax.

"Now, we have enough light in here," I mentioned as I eased myself back into my favorite chair.

"Where did you learn that? How to stick it to the plate and keep it lit?" asked Daniel.

Throwing a smug look at his brother, Zack retorted, "That's obvious. He learned it from books."

"Well, to be honest, I didn't learn this from any book. It was something your grandfather taught me." I paused. "He taught me many things, including how to survive in the wilderness."

"That's cool. So now what, we just sit here in the dark?" Daniel asked, changing the subject, a look of boredom shooting across his long face.

"What do you mean, now what?" I replied, surprised by the question. "You don't know what to do without power?"

"Not exactly," a bewildered Daniel replied.

"The cable went out a little while ago, we've got no cell service, and I can't even play the games on my phone because my battery died," Zack explained in disgust.

The tone of his voice said it all: the boys seemed lost without the luxury of electricity and modern technology. I snickered and offered them each a book. They sneered at the idea of having to read during summer vacation.

"You guys want to play a board game?" I asked with a glimmer of hope that they might say yes.

"No!" the boys replied in unison and shook their heads.

"Back when I was young, we didn't have all the electronics that you have today. Everything was different, right down to the telephone," I said.

"What do you mean the telephone was different?" asked Daniel.

I was a little taken aback by his question. I had never given it much thought that they didn't know what it was like growing up thirty years ago. "Let me explain. Phones were only found inside the home, mounted to the wall or sitting on a small table with the receivers attached to a long curly cord. You couldn't go too far from the phone when we were kids, maybe five or six feet if you were lucky. Today, all phones are just like having a personal computer in your pocket."

Outside the storm raged on; the rain came in heavy spurts and then faded to a light drizzle, alternating back and forth. We could still hear the rumbling of thunder in the distance, but it grew louder as the next wave approached. None of us knew how long the storm would last or how long the power would be out.

The boys didn't know how lucky they were to have all the luxuries they had today. I began to explain that I remembered when the first microwave ovens came out. How large they were, complete with a rotary dial knob to set the cooking time, not the small push-button type that was in our kitchen today.

I told them about black and white television sets and how we had only three or four channels to watch. VHS tapes and eight-track players were popular then, too, but they were soon replaced with cassette tapes, only to be replaced again by compact discs. Today, most of the music and movies had gone digital, even books, I explained to the boys. Things were a lot different when I was a kid.

Much to my delight, the boys seemed interested in learning about the past. They were paying attention to my story, which caught me a little by surprise.

"Would you like to hear more about my childhood, maybe even some of the wild adventures I took?" Excited, I waited for their reply.

"Sure, why not? That sounds great," both Zack and Daniel chimed in. They seemed elated to learn more about my life as a child. I could tell they didn't want to read a book or play a board game with me. I was saddened a little, but spending any one-on-one time with the boys would be great.

"Why now? Why haven't you shared any stories about your childhood before?" asked Zack.

I paused for a moment, placed my hand on my chin and briefly scratched it. "I think you're old enough now to handle some of the stories; they can be pretty scary."

"Fire away," Zack demanded as I watched both of the boys bob their heads.

I had never really taken the time to tell the boys much about my childhood. Since they appeared fascinated and I had their attention, maybe this was the perfect time to share a story or two.

Where to begin, I thought to myself. *Ah, yes...* A faint smile spread across my face. A ghost story came to mind...

"The year was 1975. I must have been about the same age as you are today, somewhere around thirteen or fourteen. I grew up in a small town in central Pennsylvania, located at the foot of the Allegheny Mountains, smack dab in the middle of nowhere, a place called Lizardville. The population was about five hundred or less, and that might be on the generous side."

"Stop, stop, stop," Zack interrupted. "So you want us to believe that you lived in a town called Lizardville. Why didn't you ever mention this before? And what kind of a name is that for a town?" The boys chuckled and laughed. All I could do was smile.

"Please, let me explain. I always thought it was a cool name. But your grandmother," I sighed and briefly paused, "well, she didn't like it, not one bit. After we grew up and moved away, she told my brother and me never to tell anyone we grew up in Lizardville. I respected my mother, so that's why I kept my mouth shut. But today, I finally share this with you." I grinned conspiratorially.

"Okay, so where was I? Oh yes..."

* * *

Growing up in Lizardville, well, things were a lot different back then. Let's go back to the beginning. A great flood hit Lizardville long before I was born, maybe even before my parents were around. There had never been much in the town, but there had been an ax factory with its large dam. The only things that survived the storm were the old dam keeper's house and another home that sat up on the side of the mountain.

The flood was so bad it left part of the Ax Factory dam in ruins. On one side of the dam, piles of rubble were all that remained; the water tore a large hole right through the base of the dam and it's still that way today. The other side escaped the force of the rushing water and remained intact. The lookout tower survived. I think because it was in the middle of the dam. The Ax Factory and the surrounding buildings were all but destroyed. After that, the property remained abandoned for years. Over time, the remaining buildings had to be torn down, leaving only the foundations.

The years passed before the state finally put the property up for sale. It was a closed bid auction. They say my parents were the only ones who bid on the dam keeper's house, so naturally they won. Next thing I knew, we were living in Lizardville.

In its glory days, the dam keeper's house sat on the banks of a beautiful lake created by the dam. Now, only swamplands surrounded the home, and on the other side of the swamp was a river called Big Fishing Creek.

Our house sat down in a valley between two small mountains, and when I say small, I mean between two and three thousand feet tall. Lots of wildlife roamed the woods: deer, bear, and porcupines, to name a few. You name it; they say it lived in those woods.

* * *

"Whoa dude, wait a minute! You're making this stuff up," Zack blurted out.

"Porcupines are dangerous? Did you ever come face to face with one? Can they throw needles from their body?" questioned Daniel.

"I've never seen one do that, and I have been pretty close to one or two in my time." I shot the boys a sly grin, making them wonder if I was hiding something. The boys nodded for me to continue. So I did…

* * *

Our place sat down on the north side of the valley floor. It was an old two-story home, built around the turn of the century, and if you counted the basement and attic, it had four levels. A small two-bedroom home with only one bathroom, there was not a lot of room when you had to share space with your older brother.

Your Uncle Buck was a year and ten days older than me. He was more than a brother or roommate. He was also my best friend. I looked up to him, even though most of the time we fought and got in trouble like we were trouble magnets or something.

Above our bedroom was the attic. Our room was the smaller of the two bedrooms, so naturally the stairway to the attic would be in our room. The basement contained three separate rooms: a cold storage room located to the right where mother kept her canned goods, on the left side was a coal room, and in the front of that was the old furnace, which made strange growling noises at night. The rest of the basement was a large, wide, open area, a great place for us to play and gather with friends. The front half of the basement was underground; the outside landscape gently sloped, exposing the back half of the basement to the backyard.

The door located in the middle of the cinderblock wall led to a backyard which was like no other. Some fifty yards away, the yard dipped into the swampy marshlands. Fireflies lit up the swamp at night. You could see hundreds of them flying around, flickering in and out. We used to catch them and keep them in a Mason jar, making homemade nightlights for our room.

The one thing we never did was venture too deep into the swamp at night, where beavers, muskrats, snakes, and other creatures lurked. Not to mention the legend of the Ax Man, who walked around looking for trespassers to cut into pieces!

* * *

"What!" Zack spat, "an Ax man?" He leaped from his chair just as another bright flash of light lit up the room. A loud crack of thunder quickly followed, sending vibrations through the window. Outside the storm raged on.

"It's just a myth," I calmly replied. I could tell Zack was still visibly shaken by the last crack of thunder. Slowly, he eased himself back in his chair and then rested his elbows on his knees. He eagerly waited for me to continue my story…

* * *

On the north side of the valley was an old two-lane road that hugged the base of the mountain. It wasn't used that much, mainly by the locals. On the south side of the valley was Big

Fishing Creek. It twisted and turned along the curves in the mountain and stretched for miles.

Your Uncle Buck and I spent much of our time in the woods, either fishing, hiking, or camping. Of course, that was when the weather was good.

Bobby Parker and his sisters, Sara and Lexi, were our closest neighbors and best friends. They lived east of our house just downstream from the dam, in the other house that survived the great flood. It was about a five-minute walk to their house. Lexi was the oldest. At sixteen, she was old enough to drive a car when her parents would let her. She didn't spend much time with our group anymore. Between working and the older boys, she hung out more in town when she had the chance. Bobby was a tall, slim boy and a year older than Buck. Sara was younger than me by a year. She was a short, thin brunette with this cute little smile that always caught my attention. She had shoulder length hair and always wore it straight down. I was glad when she finally grew out of the ribbon phase.

The five of us spent a lot of time together during the summer months. There were also a few other kids who lived nearby. Stewart Braden was an only child. A short and stocky kid with curly blond hair, the same age as me. We were even in the same class. Then there was Jimmy Brooker, who lived a little farther away, yet still within walking distance. His family lived next to the lumberyard. Jimmy was a little taller than I was and thinner. Also, he was a bit of a wild man, but I guess you could say we all had a wild side in a way. He was the same age as I was but not in the same class because he had been held back a year.

That summer a new kid arrived, Todd Hanson, who was the same age as Buck. His family bought the house next to Jimmy's down by the lumberyard. He was a stocky, well-built, dark-skinned boy. You could tell he enjoyed working out with weights. Todd came from the big city. His father took a job at the local factory, same place our dad worked. Truth be told, half the town worked there. Todd felt out of place at first. We could all understand that, having to leave all his close friends back in the city. But it didn't take long before he fit in with our little gang.

Yes, from time to time there were other kids around. Most of them lived in a small town called Mill Hall, located a few miles away, or a place called Lock Haven, just over the valley. But for the most part, it was the six of us that formed our little, no-named group of trouble makers, eight if you included the girls.

Chapter Two

There is nothing like the first weekend of summer vacation. I remember it like it was yesterday. The weather was beautiful, seventy-five degrees and not a cloud in the sky. Buck and I ran from the bus stop to the house, slamming the front door open and banging our way up the stairs to the bedroom. We never stopped to say hello to Mother, who was in the kitchen making sandwiches for lunch. Buck and I grabbed our camping gear and dashed from the room. Running downstairs, skipping steps along the way, we proceeded to check our gear to make sure we had what we needed.

"Backpack?" asked Buck.

"Check."

"Sleeping bags and tents?"

"Check, two of each, along with a pot, frying pan, and silverware, too," I added.

"Great. Do you have the fishing poles and tackle box?"

"Sure do, I think we have everything we need, except the food," I said as I glanced toward the kitchen. One thing for sure, if we had forgotten something, it would only be a short walk back to the house.

Buck, with long brown hair reaching down to his shoulders, dreamed of being a rock star. The only problem was that he didn't play any instruments, nor could he sing, trust me on that one. He enjoyed rock and roll, often playing air guitar and belting out lyrics in the safety of our room, and that would be the closest he would ever get to performing on stage.

"Boys," mother yelled from the kitchen, "your lunch is ready, just like you asked. I also have several cans of baked beans for your trip." Mother grinned, and I knew what she was thinking. If we ate baked beans and spent the entire weekend farting, she wouldn't be around to smell it.

I plopped myself down at the table next to Buck, grabbed a sandwich, and took a nice big bite. The sweet taste of the peanut butter and jelly swirled in my mouth. Grabbing my glass of milk, I washed it down. Buck snatched up his sandwich and gobbled it down one bite after another. I watched in amazement as he inhaled it like it was nothing. As I savored another bite, I thought to myself, *maybe he should slow down and enjoy it.*

I'd recently turned thirteen, had much shorter hair, and was a bit more reserved than my brother. I enjoyed school and reading, but, like most of the boys in the area, I enjoyed the refreshing sounds and smells of the great outdoors.

It wasn't long before Bobby Parker arrived at our door, wearing his signature cut-off jeans and favorite black t-shirt. We called him Parker, but not because that was his last name. It was because of what happened last summer. Parker liked to hang out at the stone quarry in the evenings. There was this large boulder located at the far end of the quarry, too large to fit in any dump truck. That was his favorite spot to chill out. He could see the entire quarry floor from there. He spent his time relaxing and gazing at the stars. He was fascinated with space and dreamed of being an astronaut when he grew up. Of course, we all knew that Parker would never be an astronaut, mainly because of his grades. At least he had a dream, unlike some of us who had no idea what we wanted to do when we got older.

One evening Parker lay in his favorite spot, enjoying the nice cool summer breeze as he gazed at the night sky. When he noticed a set of headlights coming down the road, he slid down and took cover behind one of many large mounds of gravel. Now, some of the older boys from the surrounding towns often brought their girlfriends to the quarry. It was a quiet place to park and a great place to make out. Some of us were still not interested in girls, at least not like that. But the older boys sure were. So Parker saw this car roll up not far from him and shut its lights off.

A few moments passed, and Parker became curious. He wanted to see what was going on in the car. He quietly got up and walked down to the car to take a look. He told everyone it was an old fifty-seven Chevy, a nice ride that had the back end of the car raised up or "jacked up" as the kids used to say.

Parker told us that he knew if he made any noise, the couple in the car would be startled and stop doing whatever it was they were doing. So Parker sneaked right up to the window, peeked in, and was shocked at what he saw. He told us he had never seen anything like that. He was so stunned that before he realized it, he lost his balance and struck his head against the car's window.

Now, this startled the couple in the car. Before Parker knew it, the older boy was out of the car and had knocked him to the ground and then started punching. The older boy hit him several times, he told us. It didn't take long before he was able to squirm away and get to his feet. Then he began to run. It was easy for him to get away from the other boy since the fellow had no shoes on and running on the stones would be hard on the feet. He could hear the older boy calling him a pervert as he ran away.

There was no way the other boy was going to find Parker. No one knew the quarry better than him. He said he laughed all the way home that night and that the black eye was well worth it, but he wouldn't share any more than that with us, saying we were all too young to know about things like that. He told us there was a name for the couples who came there to make out. He called them "parkers" because they parked their cars, I guess. So ever since that night, we called him Parker, just to remind him of that special night.

Parker, Buck, and I were all set to begin our weekend camping trip. We strapped on our backpacks and said goodbye to Mother as we headed out the door. It was a short walk to the dam, maybe five minutes at best.

A little ways down the road, I heard Buck holler out, "Hey, look! A soda bottle." I watched as he pulled it from the weeds. Now, bottles added up. You'd take them back to the store and get the five cent deposit back for them.

We collected all the soda bottles we could for the refund money. We already had a few hidden in the control tower at the dam. We had this special place we found located under some loose boards directly beneath one of the control panels. We'd lift them up, and buried under the floor was a large metal storage box. We stored all kinds of stuff inside, anything we wanted to keep safe or hidden from our parents. When we had enough bottles, we'd take them back to the store, and with the money, we'd buy more soda.

The three of us continued along the side of the road, kicking up the small gravel stones along the way. We didn't see any cars the entire walk. In the distance, I caught a glimpse of two figures pacing back and forth on the dam. As we got a little closer, it was easy to see that it was Stewart and Jimmy.

The dam was our playground. What remained of the dam was a ten-foot wide walkway at the base; it stood almost the same in height. The pitch of the dam made it easy to walk to the top where it opened up with another ten-foot wide walkway. It stretched a hundred yards across the valley floor, reaching to the base of the mountain. Big Fishing Creek flowed right up to it and then made its way to the south side where the dam gave way when it broke. The waters roared and swirled as it flowed around what remained of the broken down concrete structure.

Standing some twenty feet in the air, the old tower was located right in the middle of the dam. The concrete room at the top had seen better days. I was glad the stairs leading up to the top were also concrete. They looked weathered yet sturdy. The control room located at the top was the best clubhouse you could ever want. It overlooked the entire valley below. You could even see our house off in the distance along with the Parkers' home located on the side of the mountain.

The control room had several boarded up windows while others were completely missing. The old controls and electrical panels were still intact, but, of course, none of them worked. It was fun to pretend they did. Some kids had tree-houses; we had the old dam control room, a king's castle, if I say so myself. When we arrived, Buck ran upstairs to stash the soda bottle.

Stewart paced back and forth in his ratty old blue jeans and plaid shirt as he waited for the rest of us to arrive. Stewart was an only child. His mother and father worked all the time, allowing him plenty of free time to do whatever he wanted. He left them a note explaining he was going camping for the weekend. His parents would be fine with that. They bought him anything he wanted. He always had the best stuff: best tent, best sleeping bag, best all-around camping equipment we had ever seen. He was the first one of us to have a small motor scooter. That's why we called him Scooter.

On the other hand, there was Jimmy, the wild man of our group. He wore his favorite brown corduroy shorts with a stained white muscle t-shirt; his beat up sneakers showed us he wore no socks. Most of the boys wore socks pulled up to their knees, but not Jimmy. He was always different and never seemed to be afraid of anything. A daredevil of sorts, a risk taker who always accepted any challenge, even fashion. I remember one time when he found this copperhead snake, which is very poisonous. Well, Wildman Jimmy was the first to walk up to it, and before we knew it, he grabbed a stick and was playing with it. He wasn't afraid of rattlesnakes, either.

As we approached the dam, Scooter yelled out, "It's about time you slugs got here. We've been waiting for hours." We all knew that wasn't true since school had only been out for a little over an hour.

I watched as two large crows flew in and landed on the top of the tower. Sitting watching us with their beady eyes, they cawed, following our every move. Jimmy and I both glanced up and an eerie feeling sent shivers down my back.

"Have you ever seen crows that size before?" asked Jimmy.

"Not really. I guess they eat well," I chuckled.

"They're scary, don't you think?"

"I guess. I mean, they're just crows," I remember feeling a little confused by Jimmy's question. But when I think back, they were the largest crows I had ever seen in my life, and there was something about them that didn't seem right.

"Has anyone seen or heard from Todd?" I asked the group, shifting Jimmy's thoughts away from the crows.

We all looked at each other for a moment, when Scooter chimed in: "Last night he told me he would be here, he said he might be a little late. He couldn't leave until his mother got home."

The subject quickly changed. "Johnny, Scooter, Wildman, check your bags. Let me know how much food you have," demanded Parker. No one wanted to upset Parker, so we did what he asked. After all, he was the leader of our little group.

We each held up three cans of beans. "Great, each of you owes me one can of beans," he shouted. "You had better hope you can catch some fish if you want to eat. Either that or die of starvation. And if you die, I'll have to feed you to the bears."

Parker laughed, followed by Buck, who also demanded a can from each of us troops.

We all played along and handed them each a can of beans as requested. I knew Scooter did all the cooking, and we only had one pot to cook in. So the beans would be cooked together and divided between the six of us.

What felt like an hour was only twenty minutes before Todd finally arrived. We spotted him walking alongside the road, making his way toward the dam. I thought it was odd that he wasn't carrying anything. No bag, no tent, flat out nothing. How was he going to survive the weekend with no gear?

"Hi guys," Todd said as he approached waving his hand.

"Where's your gear? You're not going, are you?" quizzed Parker.

"I don't own any camping gear. You guys remember I'm from the city." Todd gave them a sly grin. "This is my first camping trip. I didn't know I needed to bring anything. I did borrow some cigarettes from my older brother. I'm willing to share if I can stay in someone's tent," he said as he pulled them from his front pocket. None of us smoked, but the older boys might try it.

"That sounds great, man." Parker's smile grew big. "Scooter has the biggest tent. You can stay with him," he added.

Out of the corner of my eye, I noticed the two large crows had taken flight and were circling above like vultures waiting for a meal. The six of us began to pick up our gear as the crows swooped down, catching us all by surprise. They passed just over our heads, cawing loudly as they barely missed us. Scooter hit the deck and lay flat on the concrete; Jimmy took off his ball hat and waved it at the birds as they passed. The others ducked as I did, but they didn't give the birds much attention. Not like Jimmy, Scooter, or I did.

"What the hell is wrong with those crows?" Jimmy yelled as he tried to find a small rock to throw at them. "They seem to be following me," he nervously stated.

"Who knows? Just grab your gear and let's hit the trail," Parker said and smiled.

I watched as the crows landed back on the tower. They seemed fixed on Jimmy for some reason. Jimmy finally found a small rock and tossed in their direction, but his throw came up short.

We all grabbed our packs and placed them on our backs. Todd grabbed two of the sleeping bags to help lighten the load for Parker and Buck since he had nothing else to carry. Our group slowly walked to the edge of the dam. We stopped once to look around to make sure we hadn't forgotten anything. Then we continued into the swamp, down one of many dirt paths that led to Big Fishing Creek. Now, don't get me wrong, the swamp had plenty of water in it, but it also had a lot of dirt trails too. The local sportsmen who fished the creek created many of the paths. They were pretty clear this time of the year. We weren't the foolish type of kids to go jumping into the swampy waters. No, we stayed on the dirt paths when we could.

We made our way to the creek and walked along until the water had slowed as we searched for a great place to fish and set up camp. The sounds of the rushing water faded, and everything had become more peaceful and quiet. Birds were chirping, and the bees were buzzing. Those were the only sounds I heard. We continued walking, listening to branches break under our feet with every step. I had already forgotten about the rest of the world.

We were chatting away and making all kinds of noise like boys do. When we came around a bend in the path, Parker stopped and knelt down, balling his hand into a fist and then raising it straight in the air, our signal to halt. "Be quiet," he whispered as we suddenly came to a stop. What had Parker heard? The moment was tense, right before Jimmy screamed.

The sudden sound of his yell caught us all off guard. I jumped as many others did. Jimmy had played a prank, laughter quickly erupted. My nerves were still recovering when we all heard a different noise. Crackle! Snap! Branches began breaking all around us. I tensed up again, and so did the others. Three deer leaped across the path, dashed into the open field, and then quickly vanished. We were all startled; my heart pounded like a bass drum. None of us had even seen the deer. We would have walked right past if Parker hadn't stopped. Parker always had a keen eye. After all, he lived in the area the longest and knew the woods like the back of his hand.

"Are you crazy, Jimmy?" Parker yelled. "I told you all to stop and be quiet. You could have got us all killed."

"Don't be a spaz," Jimmy interrupted. "I was only kidding around," Jimmy spat back, and then he started laughing. We all lost it the minute Jimmy snorted. That was it for me, too. I laughed so hard that tears rolled down my cheeks.

"Yeah, well, in your face, deadhead," Parker replied and turned his back to Jimmy and the rest of us.

"Let's just book it. We'll leave the douche bags here and see how they fare on their own," Buck whispered to Parker.

"Yeah, you're right, man. Let's move on."

"Oh, lighten up, dudes," Todd snapped back. "It's all good. We're just having a little fun, and to be frank, those deer scared the crap out of me."

"By the way, did you all see the look on Johnny's and Scooter's faces? Those deer freaked 'em out, man. I thought they were gonna mess their pants," Buck said laughing before moving down the path.

"We were fine," I barked back as I picked up my gear. We cautiously continued on our journey, hoping nothing else would jump out of the woods. Then Jimmy noticed an old tin can lying along the dirt path.

I frowned. "It's sad that some folks have to leave trash out here." Maybe this was just some old can a fisherman used to carry bait. Or maybe someone enjoyed a nice can of beans over an open fire. But the fact remained, it wasn't nice to leave trash in the woods. After all, we thought of the woods as our second home.

"Yeah, I'm sure it's something you left here last year," Jimmy said, shoving me in the shoulder.

23

"You chump," I spat as I pushed him back. We pushed and shoved each other a few times as we walked down the path, without a care in the world.

Parker and Buck continued to walk ahead of the rest of the pack. I wondered if they were thinking they were on a secret military patrol, searching for the enemy. The Vietnam War had just ended, and it was something that was still fresh on everyone's mind. They continued to walk a little farther before they realized we were no longer behind them. Knowing Buck, I'm sure he thought we had wimped out under the weight of our backpacks. "What a bunch of sissies," I heard Parker yell in the distance. We heard footsteps quickly approaching and could tell they had raced back to us. As they turned the corner, they spotted us sitting on our backpacks.

Parker sighed. "Are you girls done messing around?"

"Yeah, just taking a small break," I said as Jimmy and I picked up our gear. "Let's move out!" I snapped to attention and saluted Parker.

Jimmy quickly kicked the can a few yards in front of him. Scooter joined in, and the two played kick the can for the next twenty minutes, laughing and having a good old time.

We continued down the path another thirty minutes until we reached a spot that was several miles deep into the woods. To us boys, it felt more like a hundred miles. We came to a small round clearing next to the creek. What a great spot for our camp. There was a pool of water that slowly swirled near the bottom of the rapids. The main part of the stream veered to the left side, going away from the camp. A large tree had fallen over the pooled area and stretched out over part of the creek. It seemed like a perfect place to hide if you were a fish. There was enough room for three or four of us to fish in that area. And it was clear of debris, so the chance of our lines getting hung up or stuck on something was minimal, as long as we didn't cast our fishing lines directly into the branches of the downed tree.

Jimmy put his gear down and quickly set out in search of large rocks, hoping to find some close to the size of cinder blocks. One by one, he brought them back to camp and placed them in the center of the clearing to form a circle. Scooter pulled a small, fold-up shovel from his backpack and began to dig a large hole in the middle of the rocks. The fire pit would be about a foot deep and about four feet in diameter. Jimmy placed the large rocks around the outer edge of the pit to complete the circle.

I showed Todd what we had to do before we could set up the tents. Together, we cleared small branches and rocks on the forest floor, tossing them away from where we would place the tents. "It's hard to get a good night's sleep if you're sleeping on branches or rocks," I explained.

Todd began to hum as he worked. The tune grew louder and louder, and then he put words to it. One by one, we all joined in. It was a song we all loved and knew well, "Taking Care of Business" by BTO, Bachman–Turner Overdrive.

We sang as we worked, making sure the tents weren't too close to the fire. Todd and I worked together and set up the first tent. Several minutes later, I pulled out my tent as Todd began working on one by himself. Soon, all five tents were up and formed a large half-circle around the fire pit. Then we placed sleeping bags and other personal stuff inside each tent, which included making sure Buck and Parker each had their extra food supplies.

While we all set up camp, Buck ventured off into the forest, reappearing every few minutes with his arms full of wood. Soon, the smell of smoke wafted around the camp, and the crackle of the flames rang out. We would need plenty to keep the fire burning all night. The last thing we wanted was a bear or bobcat coming to pay us a visit in the middle of the night.

Parker unpacked his backpack and placed his junk in the tent. Then we took inventory of all our supplies, counting fifteen cans of baked beans, one bag of marshmallows, a stick of butter, and six candy bars that Parker had "borrowed" from the local gas station.

He noticed we didn't have anything to drink. Thank goodness the creek water was clean and cold. Parker tossed a few canteens at me. I carried them to the water's edge and began filling them with the cool mountain water.

Thirty minutes had passed since we arrived at the camp. It was approaching late afternoon. We had only an hour, maybe two, to get some fishing done before nightfall. We gathered our fishing gear, and Parker and Buck walked upstream to see if they were biting on the upper side of the rapids. Todd went with Jimmy and me because he didn't have any experience when it came to fishing. The training always seemed to fall to us younger boys, so as not to disrupt the older guys. It wasn't long before we cast our lines into the clear blue water that swirled below the rapids.

I remember my first toss. It was perfect. I watched it fall just below the branches. No sooner had the line broken the water's surface than it was yanked downward. I quickly pulled back and upward. I had hooked the fish or whatever it was on the other end. "Yes," I whispered to myself as I stood up and backed away from the water's edge. My line darted to the left and then dove deep into the water. Suddenly, the line went in the other direction, diving deeper. There was too much slack in the line, so the fish quickly came back toward the surface and leaped out, splashing around when it landed back in the water. The fish continued swirling around; it looked to be a good size trout. I reeled as fast as I could, removing all slack from the line and keeping the fish on the other end. After a few more minutes, the fish tired and the battle was over. I finally reeled it to shore. Todd stood by with the net and scooped up a nice, fourteen-inch, brown trout.

* * *

"Wait a minute," Daniel snapped, "You were the first one to catch a fish?"

I could tell by the look in his eyes that he didn't believe me. "Hey, this is my story, and if I'm telling it, then by golly, I'll be the first one to catch a fish. And the biggest one too, I might add," I said with a grin as I tried to convince them I was telling the truth.

"Okay, Dad, it's your story. Tell it as you will," said Zack.

"Yeah sure, Dad," Daniel chimed in. "I'm not sure if your story is even true at this point."

"Well, it's my fish story." I snickered. "Now where was I. Oh, yes."

* * *

Scooter walked a little ways downstream and hadn't even cast his line in before I had reeled in the first catch of the day. We all fished until night fell. Buck and Parker had come back with four each, a nice mix of brown, speckled, and rainbow trout. Jimmy, Todd, and I had each caught two, and Scooter pulled in a total of six. Not bad for the first night.

Jimmy, Todd, and I drew fish cleaning detail. We gutted and filleted some of the fish. We threw the fish guts back in the water and cleaned the knives and rocks to reduce the smell of blood and guts in an effort not to attract wild animals.

Caw, Caw, one of the large crows squawked while watching us from the tree top on the other side of the creek. Jimmy noticed it first, and then he motioned to me. We exchanged stares with the crows. We tried to finish cleaning our fish before they came over and tried to steal our food.

"I've never seen crows that size before," Jimmy said.

I scratched my head a bit trying to figure it out. Then I nodded in agreement. I didn't even know they were there and watching us from a distance. They never moved. They only observed. Something was different about these birds. I couldn't put a finger on it at the time. I stood up and took the fillets over to Scooter. They seemed to be following us, but I knew better because crows don't follow people, or do they?

We left the remaining fish that we didn't gut in the fishing basket. Before submerging the small wooden cage into the water just enough so we could see the top of it sticking out of the water, I fastened the cage to a nylon rope and wrapped the other end around the base of a small tree next to the shoreline. By keeping the fish alive, we would have plenty of fresh fish for breakfast because no one had thought to bring any eggs.

Scooter had finished prepping the fire as he poured four cans of baked beans into a large metal pot. He then placed it over the fire by using a potholder he had made out of two large branches. With his shovel, he moved some of the hot coals from the center of the fire to the edge by the rocks and then placed the frying pan on top the red-hot coals, making sure to keep the pan off the open flames.

"Tonight, we'll be eating like kings," Scooter bragged as he flipped the fish in the frying pan.

Dinner was ready, and in no time at all, we were chowing down on fish and beans.

Chapter Three

We gathered around the fire as darkness fell over the forest. The sound of crickets chirping filled the air. The moon, now stretching into the night sky, cast an eerie glow upon the forest floor. We laughed and told stories while sitting on these large logs that Buck had rolled into camp earlier that day. Todd broke out the cigarettes, with only Parker and Buck taking one. The rest of us were too young, the older boys suggested. Scooter smiled because he didn't want to try one, and neither did I. Jimmy was the only one who seemed a little upset.

Jimmy told everyone an interesting story. It was about a wild dog, or maybe a pack of wild dogs, I don't remember. We could never tell whether or not his stories were true. He said the dogs were running around the lumberyard stealing lunches from the workers. Some of the workers blamed him for taking the food, but he swore he had nothing to do with it. He hinted he had seen the dogs himself and so had some of the other workers, but none of us had ever seen a wild dog in the area. Just like a lot of what Jimmy said, you had to take it with a grain of salt. My guess, Jimmy was the one taking the lunches.

We went around the campfire, each taking a turn to tell a story. Some true I'm sure; others, probably not. Then it was Bobby Parker's turn to tell his story.

"So, Todd, tell me, have you heard about the legend of the Ax man?" asked Parker.

Todd gave him a funny look and then glanced around at the rest of us to see if Parker was trying to pull a fast one. By the looks of things, he could tell Parker was serious for once.

"No, I don't think I have," he responded.

The clouds began to roll in, hiding the moon and casting a dark shadow over the forest. A cool breeze whipped through the trees, sending a fresh chill in the air. A great horned owl hooted nearby and was answered by another owl off in the distance. We looked over our shoulders as paranoia began to set in. One at a time, we leaned forward trying to get a better spot to hear Parker's ghost story.

"Back around the turn of the century, there used to be the old Ax Factory located right here in Lizardville. If I remember right, it was named SE Tool Company, which stood for Sharpe... Edge ...Tools," Parker barked. What Todd didn't know was that Parker was an excellent story teller, filled with plenty of emotion and hand gestures.

"Some of the older folks in town call this the Old Dam site, others call it the Ax Mann dam, but the oldest of the town folk call it the old Ax Factory dam. No matter how you say it today, it's still the "old dam of death" to me." Parker slowly gazed at each of us, making eye contact before moving to the next person. "This place has claimed many a lives over the years, from murders, suicides, and even people drowning in the creek. Death surrounds us tonight, boys."

Almost on cue, a giant gust of wind blew, rustling the branches above us and sending a few leaves floating to the ground. I felt a chill run down my spine, and from the looks of the others faces, I wasn't the only one who had that feeling. Parker had our full attention.

"If this place is so dangerous and surrounded by death, then why in God's name are we spending the night out here?" Todd asked.

"Because," Parker hesitated, "we're not afraid of anything!" He paused again, looking directly at Todd, and asked, "Are you?"

Parker received no verbal response from Todd, only a slight nod and a blank stare. Parker continued with his story. "See, back when the factory was in its prime, there were several buildings located here that made up the factory complex. There was a large warehouse building where most of the finished hatchets and axes were stored, a small office building and a garage building where they kept a delivery truck or horse and carriages along with the maintenance gear, and a military barracks-style building that housed the workers who didn't live nearby. But the largest building of all was the factory itself. Over a hundred people worked there.

"Just north of the dam, located at the base of the mountain, was a small house that was owned by the plant manager and his wife. Today that house is owned by my family." Parker smiled. "That's why I know so much about the old legends."

"They used to make the axes that supplied the local woodsmen, even the military when they needed supplies. They cut the logs from the forest, dragged them to the creek, and floated them down to the dam where they were gathered, and then cut into long planks. They used the wood to make the handles for the axes. The steel plants near Pittsburg supplied them with large pieces of steel, which they used to make the fine blades. Some say they made picks and shovels, too.

"The place was full of life, making hundreds of axes a day. It was hard work, hot in the summer and cold in the winter.

"Legend has it that one cool evening in June, a night just like tonight," he paused to take a deep breath, "everything changed. Nothing was ever the same after that night. The entire area suffered from the events of one evening. It almost turned this town into a ghost town."

"What happened?" Scooter asked nervously. The sound of crickets chirping could be heard in the background.

Parker cautiously looked around for a few seconds before he continued with dramatic flair: "A spring thunderstorm had rolled in, the skies rumbled, the winds howled, and the rains poured. It was a miserable night.

"At six o'clock, the blaring sound of a horn filled the air. The day shift had ended. Sitting in his home, the owner stood, putting on his trench coat and boots. It was time to make his way over to the factory to check on the night shift that had just arrived.

"As the men filed out of the factory, one person stood out. A tall, young, handsome man, in his mid-twenties, he had just finished his shift and was heading to town for a few drinks with his buddies. As he left the plant, he glanced toward the hillside where he noticed the owner's wife standing alone in the front window of the house. She gazed into the storm. He couldn't help but wonder if she was looking for someone.

"She was a tall, beautiful woman, much younger than her husband, by some twenty years. Rumor has it that she only married him for his money. Her blonde hair flowed past her shoulders. She had the prettiest blue eyes and a smile that could light up any room. She was all alone in the house. The young man's interest was piqued as he remembered his days in high school when he and the young woman were a couple. It didn't seem like that long ago, but it had been a few years. Something churned inside the man, a feeling he could not explain. He wanted to see her, to hold her, to be close to her once again.

"He turned to his friends, telling them to go on without him, saying he had forgotten something and would catch up in a little while. As his friends made their way toward town, he backtracked toward the factory and stepped behind a large tree, waiting for the old man to pass. Soon, he heard footsteps sloshing in the rain-soaked field. He went unnoticed as the old fellow quickly made his way up the steep embankment toward the factory. Now was the young man's chance; he knew the old man would be gone for at least an hour. He just wanted to say hi and see how she was doing. He turned and quickly made his way across a vacant lot. Then, as he slowed his pace, he stopped and stood in the rain. Dripping wet, he watched her gaze out the window.

"*Annabelle,* he thought to himself. *What a wonderful life we could have shared if I had only waited for her.* He knew deep down what he was about to do was wrong, but something inside possessed him. A feeling he could not contain. He stepped onto the sidewalk and stopped as he stared at the window one last time. He thought to himself, *'You need to walk away, it's not too late. She's not your wife.'* He knew he had his chance and had blown it.

"Just as he started to leave, she noticed him, and their eyes met for the first time since high school. In that very moment, he could sense she felt the same way. She disappeared from the window, and he wondered if she was afraid, but then she opened the door. Standing before him was his beautiful Annabelle in her long white dress. He took a few steps up on the porch and then stopped. Her lavender scent filled the air, a smell he remembered vividly from the times they had spent together.

"She stepped forward, as did he, and he took her into his arms, and a warm, wonderful feeling rushed over him. It felt great to hold her again, to feel the softness of her skin against his. The smell of her shampoo awakened his senses. Truly, her love intoxicated him. She soon backed away as she held out her hand, their fingers now intertwined. Then she pulled him into the home and, with his foot, he closed the door behind them."

Everyone stared at Parker; the flames from the fire flickered and danced on the surrounding bushes. The atmosphere was hypnotic. The trees seemed to leap out as the branches swayed in the wind, and the shadows from the fire raced across the leaves. None of us paid attention to the approaching storm that was heading our way. The wind continued to increase, and the temperature dropped, sending goose bumps over my body. No one noticed the rustling sound in the bushes behind us as Parker continued with his story.

"Annabelle pulled the handsome young man into the room. He gently lifted her up, sat her on the edge of the table, and pressed his body into hers. She wrapped her legs around him and pulled him closer. Her soft lips met his for the first time in many years, and they began to kiss. A hot burning feeling rushed through his body.

"All of the sudden, the front door burst open, crashing against the wall creating a loud BANG!" Parker shouted, making all of us jump.

"Ah, man! You scared the crap out of me!" I shouted as I jumped to my feet.

"Yeah, you're a real low life," hollered Scooter. A few of the others quietly grumbled in an effort to hide the fact that they were a little bit frightened.

"Just making sure you cats are paying attention," chimed Parker as he watched us all sit back down on the logs. He waited a bit and then cleared his throat.

"The old man had returned home earlier than expected, holding a large ax in his right hand as he entered the room. Anger and adrenaline filled his veins as he looked at Annabelle and her young lover.

"The young man spun around and tried to explain. Annabelle shivered at the sight of her husband and backed away. A devastating hatred came over the old man as he darted across the floor, swinging the ax to the right and then to the left as he struck the young man over and over.

"The thunder roared outside, covering up the screams from inside the home. The young man crumbled to his knees before the old man, begging and pleading for him to stop. Filled with rage, or supernatural power, the old man struck him again and again. Everything happened so fast that the young man never had a chance to defend himself against the deadly blows from the ax.

"Horrified, Annabelle stood helpless as she watched. Not knowing what to do, she screamed for help and then cried as she watched her husband beat her young lover to death. She knew she was partly to blame; she had been wrong to invite the man into her home.

"His body lay on the floor covered in blood. Annabelle collapsed beside him as she wrapped her arms around the lifeless body. She ran her hands up his chest and then to his face. Quickly, she pulled her hand back, his warm blood dripping from her fingers.

"The old man stepped back and threw the ax across the room in disgust. He was stunned at what he had done in a moment of madness. He sighed at Annabelle and tried to comfort her, but she wanted nothing to do with him. He quickly became angry, yelling, screaming, and blaming her for his actions. He ran to the bedroom and pulled a blanket from the closet. He returned, knelt over the body, and began to roll it inside the blanket. The old man was strong as he hoisted the bundle over his shoulder. He instructed Annabelle to clean up the mess and that he would quickly return.

"Carrying the body out the back of the house and stopping briefly at the shed to grab a small shovel and lantern, he closed the door and walked the lone dirt path that led deep into the mountains to dispose of the quickly stiffening body. He had once found a cavern, an isolated place deep in the woods that only he knew about. When he arrived there, he dug a shallow grave and placed the body into the hole. After covering the hole, he scattered leaves and branches over the dirt to give it a natural look. He laid the shovel to the side. A strange feeling rushed over the old man that sent unexplainable chills up his spine.

"Wet and covered in mud, he turned and began his long journey back. He had been gone for several hours when he spotted the soft glow of light shining through the rain. He hurried his pace before pushing the back door open. He walked across the kitchen, leaving a trail of muddy footprints when he noticed the floor in the dining room was not clean. Deep red blood stained the floors, and splatter marks lined the walls. He looked around and called for Annabelle. Had she left, possibly gone into town to report him? The thought crossed his mind. Panic set in as he realized there was no way he was going to get away with this.

"But what could he do now? His mind raced; the deed was already done. He entered the bedroom and quickly froze in his tracks. That's when he spotted Annabelle, swinging from the rafters. Her beautiful, lifeless body, suspended in midair, a bed sheet wrapped around her neck. A broken chair lay beneath her. He was stunned and at a loss for words. He fell to his knees and cried out as she hung before him. Several moments had passed before he gained the strength and was able to stand. Stepping up to the bed, he pulled out his pocket knife, took Annabelle in his arms, gently cut away the sheet, and lowered her motionless body on the bed. He unraveled the sheet from around her neck to reveal deep red burn marks.

"Alone and distraught, he knew he had only one option left. He couldn't live without his Annabelle. Slowly, he walked toward a small nightstand beside his bed. Opening a drawer, he pulled out a pistol. Without hesitating, he placed the barrel alongside his head, pulled the trigger, and instantly collapsed to the floor."

"Oooh… you're joshing me," were the words that flew out of Todd's mouth as he jumped to his feet and threw his hands to the air. "Ah, that's crazy man." He continued his rant.

I snickered, watching Todd dance around.

Slowly, he calmed himself down, and then looked around the camp. He glanced at Buck, whose eyes shone larger than life, so much so, he looked to be in a trance. He said nothing. Then Todd glanced at me; I gazed back with my jaw hanging wide open, my head swaying in disbelief. A quick glance at Scooter and then Jimmy told him everyone was deeply entrenched in Parker's story.

Todd realized that everyone was as stunned as he was; however, he was the only one jumping around in disbelief. Then it hit him like a ton of bricks. "Your story can't be true," he challenged Parker.

"Oh, but it is," Parker responded. "See, my family bought the house where the murders took place. The very same house indeed," said Parker, giving Todd a convincing nod. "My grandfather got a great deal on the home because no one wanted to buy a haunted house. After he had passed away, he left the house to my father, who added a few more rooms and the garage. That's why it doesn't look the same as it did back then. But rest assured it's the same house, and the stories are true."

"Before my grandfather passed away, he shared the story with me. He said when he was a kid someone had found an old diary in the house that Annabelle's sister used to own, the house where she raised Annabelle's daughter. The police said the book belonged to her and contained detailed information about the events of that night, stuff that only the daughter would know since she was the only one in the house at the time when the killings happened. She witnessed everything that night, even her mother's suicide, and she wrote about it in her journal. The police reopened the case, and they searched the mountains again for several weeks. Still they found nothing," said Parker.

Todd nodded as if he approved, and so did the rest of us.

The wind swirled around the treetops. We could hear the thunder in the distance, this being the first time that any of us even noticed the approaching storm.

"I think there's a storm coming," I said gravely.

"Yeah right, you're always worried about that kind of crap," Buck said as he turned to Parker. "So what happened next?"

Chapter Four

Parker glanced at Buck, then at the rest of us. "This is what happened next," he said. "The next morning some of the workers noticed the old man didn't take his morning stroll through the factory. They began to talk amongst themselves. Some of the young man's friends even wondered what had happened to him the night before since he never showed up at the tavern, not to mention he wasn't at work that morning."

"No kidding," Jimmy yelled out and began to laugh. Scooter and I joined in.

"You clowns done yet? If you don't want to know how it ends, just say so. I'll stop," Parker barked in an angry tone. "May I continue?"

Silence fell over the camp as we gazed at one another. Several of us spoke at once. "All right, man, go ahead, finish your story."

Parker thought for a moment and then continued. "The workers began to get worried. Some of them knew the young man and Annabelle had been high school sweethearts. After much discussion, a few of the men decided to go and check on the boss and his family.

"The group walked across the dam, making their way to the home. As they approached, they noticed the front door was slightly open. An uneasy feeling settled over them not knowing what lay beyond the door. They weren't sure if they should enter the house or send someone to alert the authorities. 'What if something happened to the family? What if they need our help?' one of them asked."

"You're presuming they're still alive," said one of the others.

"I hope nothing horrible has happened to the family," another remarked.

"Times a wasting, boys," another fellow mentioned. They all knew it would take an hour if someone went to town, possibly two before they would return with help. After a little more conversation, one of them decided to look inside, even if it meant finding a bunch of dead bodies.

"The group slowly walked up on the porch. Stopping at the front door, one man took a deep breath, then slowly pushed the door open.

"They found… NOTHING," Parker yelled. Then he watched and laughed while the rest of us jumped out of our skin.

"Dude, you're sick," said Buck as he threw a marshmallow at Parker hitting him in the chest.

Parker raised his hands to deflect several marshmallows that came his way. I guess everyone decided to throw one instead of eating them.

"I think he's had enough," said Buck, motioning for him to continue.

After clearing his throat, Parker went on. "They pushed the door open. A loud creaking sound came from the rusty old hinges. They peered into the room and noticed it was empty. A foul stench hung in the air, one that hurt the senses. Quickly, they all began to catch a whiff of the odor. The smell of death they presumed, cupping their hands over their mouths and noses.

"Right inside the house, one of the men noticed the blood splattered on the walls and the bloody ax that lay on the far side of the room. A large pool of dried blood was on the floor near the table. Then he saw some blood sprayed all over the furniture. Even though he didn't see any bodies, he knew something bad had happened. He wondered if they had crawled to the bedroom. *Something happened in here all right, but what,* the man thought to himself. He hollered, 'Is anyone home?' There was no answer. 'I'm coming in. I'm only here to help.'

"Taking a few more steps inside the house, he got a better look around. He could see there had been a struggle. He called out to his buddies who were waiting on the porch. As he walked carefully, he kept his back pushed tight against the entrance wall, making sure not to step in any of the mess or touch anything he shouldn't as he walked toward the front bedroom. He glanced around the corner and noticed another pool of blood located near the foot of the bed. A small handgun lay on the floor. He wondered what the gun was doing there. Next he spotted a knotted up sheet lying at the foot of the bed. Part of it had been cut off. He glanced upward at the rafter and made the connection. The nasty smell of urine stained the bed.

"The second man entered the bedroom. They gazed at each other and wondered what had happened here. Had the young man who worked at the plant killed the mister and misses? If so, where were the bodies? A third man came into the house and joined the two in the bedroom. They all turned to one another; none of this made any sense. The three of them left the bedroom and made their way to the kitchen.

"From the kitchen doorway, they noticed muddy footprints on the floor. They appeared to start on the far side of the room by the back door that led outside. From the direction of the muddy shoe prints, someone had entered the house there. Then they walked toward the living room; the prints came to a halt in the master bedroom where the floor was covered by a rug. From the looks of it, the person who entered the house stopped only once to look around.

"Had some stranger passing through town happened to take the family? Where were the bodies? What about the young man? Did he have something to do with this? They soon realized one of them had to notify the police.

"An hour later, the police arrived. They searched the house from top to bottom. Then they searched the woods located behind the home. They even had all the factory workers and many town folks join the search as they walked the woods. They searched for a few days, even along the creek. The story goes that they never found any of the bodies."

Parker slowly turned and glanced around the camp. "They say that Annabelle still walks these woods today in search of her young lover. She carries the very ax that killed him."

The moon vanished behind the dark clouds hidden in the night sky. The storm grew closer as the top of the trees swayed back and forth, sending a few branches and leaves to the ground. Scooter nervously looked around. It was too dark to see anything beyond the firelight.

The snapping of branches and rustling in the bushes caught our attention. Some strange sounds were coming from the woods. I stood up and turned around. I wasn't sure what I heard behind me. "It's just the wind," I said in an unsettling voice. I heard a low growl off in the distance. "Was that a growl? Something's growling out there!" I said, now a little panicked.

Buck stood up and peered into the woods. "We should check it out," he said and took a step forward.

"I'm not getting any good vibes, man. I'm staying right here," said Scooter as he shook his head.

"Scaredy-cat," Jimmy yelled, jumping to his feet and taking a few steps toward the woods. Parker quickly bounced to his feet as something scurried across the forest floor and made its way through the bushes. Both of them came to a halt. Jimmy took a few steps back and turned to look at the rest of us around the camp; we were all standing on our feet now. Buck and Parker stood in the same spot, frozen like a couple of statues.

"Something's out there," said Todd, nervously.

Not knowing what to do, we all stood in silence. Pop… crackle… sounds of branches breaking in the forest sent us all scurrying around looking for something to use as a weapon.

Scooter and I both grabbed thick branches that were about two feet in length. Todd and Jimmy picked up some of the larger stones that had encircled the fire and quickly tossed them to the ground because they were too hot to hold. Buck and Parker stood the closest to the woods, wondering what was just beyond their sight. More branches snapped, and then a loud moan rang out. It was a woman's voice.

"That was no animal," hissed Buck.

"Whatever or whoever is out there better show your face now," Parker hollered.

"Last warning!" Todd yelled as he stepped forward and began swinging a small branch back and forth in front of him.

"What if it's a black bear? What if he smelled the fish?" I asked, looking around at the others.

Everyone froze again, blank stares on our faces.

"Set some branches on fire. Bears are afraid of fire," barked Jimmy.

"They're also afraid of noise. Everyone yell!" shouted Parker.

We all stood around the fire briefly looking at one another, and then one by one, we started yelling as loud as we could to scare the bear away. What a sight, six boys standing around a campfire, yelling at the top of their lungs. It was a good thing we didn't have cell phones back then, or the video would have ended up on YouTube.

Finally, Parker waved his hands back and forth, signaling us to stop the screaming so we could listen. "That should do it if it's a bear. But what if it's Annabelle?" Parker said, looking left and then right, staring at each of us. "What if she's here to kill us?"

The wind howled, sending a flurry of leaves falling all around us as they drifted down from the sky. More branches broke, and a rustling sound came from the bushes followed by another moan. The sound was coming from right in front of us, loud thrashing sounds, like someone swinging an ax or a machete was cutting through the bushes making his way toward the camp. More whacking sounds, back and forth, were followed by a loud scream as not one, but two ragged looking females came bursting out of the woods screaming, yelling, and running directly toward us.

Scooter screamed instinctively, turned, and ran to the creek. The one thing I had learned about survival was that you only had to be faster than one other person to survive an attack, so I was not far behind. I made a beeline for a large tree and started to climb. I hoped ghosts couldn't climb trees. I scurried up the tree, looked back, and that's when I noticed it wasn't Annabelle at all. It was Lexi and Sara. Feeling a little embarrassed, I began to make my way down the tree. I always wanted to be the tough guy in front of Sara, yet I had run away like a scaredy-cat.

Buck, Parker, and Jimmy had all stood their ground, but they looked a little shaky. They were prepared to fight. I watched as they grabbed logs that were lying in the fire. They were about to swing the flaming end at their attackers when they suddenly realized it was Parker's sisters.

"Are you crazy? We could have killed you," Jimmy blurted out.

"What the hell!" yelled Parker. "Are you two nuts? Does Mom know you're out here?" He was furious with his sisters for trying to scare us.

Lexi was Parker's older sister. She didn't pay any attention to his comment. "Little Bobby-boy, who do you think sent us out here, huh? It was Mom; she was thinking her little boy might get all wet and wash away with the storm coming in."

"Go home and tell Mom we can take care of ourselves. We don't need you checking up on us," Parker spat back.

Buck laughed. "Hey, sunshine, that was good. You had us going for a minute."

Lexi cracked a wry smile at Buck and then shot him a wink.

At this point, I had made my way down from the tree and walked back to the camp while Scooter peeked from behind the tree next to the water's edge. "If Parker hadn't been telling his story, we wouldn't have been so jumpy," I explained.

Todd had never left camp. Everything had happened so fast, he never reacted. He just stood in the same spot. "That was sick… You scared the crap out of us because of Parker's ghost … ah," Todd slowed his speech and stopped midsentence. His eyes met Lexi's for the first time. He had never met Parker's sister until that very moment. Lexi was slim and taller than any of the boys. Her long legs and almost perfect body caught his attention immediately. Her long blonde curls blocked part of her face. She reached up and brushed them away with a stroke of her hand. His eyes glazed over as he noticed her beautiful lips and stunning blue eyes. Todd made a funny face. Once again, he tried to speak, but something weird happened. "Ah…

hi… there, I'm Toad… I mean, I, aaaah. I move just here, aaaah, from Spits-burg," he stammered, so embarrassed that his face turned red. He quickly tried to gain his composure by clearing his throat and sticking his chest out.

"Wow… Spits-burg… huh? I have never met anyone from Spits-burg before," Lexi laughed. "Tell me, Toad. What's it like in Spits-burg?" she said. Then she winked and gave him a cute smile.

I could understand what he was trying to say, yet the right words couldn't find their way out of his mouth. I don't think he knew what was happening to him; then he tried to speak again. This time, he looked determined to get it right: "I, um… what, no idea, trying say. Ugg." His mind and mouth couldn't get the words right as he bowed his head, turned, and sat down on the log.

I couldn't help but laugh because Todd had made a complete fool of himself in front of Lexi. It was then that I noticed Sara staring at me. I blushed and didn't know what to say either. The only word that came out of my mouth was "hi," with a little wave of my hand.

"Hello," giggled Sara.

"Are we done looking like a bunch of chumps?" Buck snarled, looking directly at Todd and then to me. He turned his attention to the girls. "Nice of you to try and scare the crap out of us," said Buck.

"To be honest, Mom never asked us to come out here. We saw the fire and knew right where to find you. As we got closer, we could hear Bobby telling one of his ghost's stories.

We already had on old clothes, and it seemed only right to teach you boys a lesson, so we messed up our hair and smeared a little dirt on our faces," smiled Lexi, flirting with Buck as she twirled her curls between her fingers.

"Well, you got us this time, but you better watch your back 'cause paybacks are hell," Parker snarled with an evil grin as he nudged his sister.

One by one, we settled down and took our seats around the campfire. Todd gave up his spot to Lexi, and Sara sat next to her. The storm seemed to be passing to the north, and we hadn't received any rain, just a little wind. Sitting around the fire, we roasted marshmallows and shared more stories.

A little while later, Todd's curiosity must have gotten the best of him. He blurted out, "So, why didn't they ever find the bodies?"

"I don't know, man, they just never did. Some say Annabelle still walks these woods today seeking revenge," warned Parker.

"I find your story a little hard to believe," says Todd.

"Well, that's your choice, dude."

"Ssssh, did you hear that?" said Parker, raising his finger to his lips for everyone to be quiet.

All we could hear was the crackle of the fire. We looked at one another for a few moments and then gazed into the woods. It was too dark to see anything beyond our fire.

"I don't hear anything. Whatever it was must be gone," says Buck.

"Maybe you're right," agreed Jimmy.

There it was again, the loud cracking sound of a branch breaking, only twenty yards away from camp. I think we all heard it at the same time, we sat up straight and began to look around. Sara nudged Lexi, who responded by shaking her head as if she didn't know what the sound was. Parker laid his branch next to the fire to make a torch. Buck and Jimmy did the same. Scooter was ready to run again as was I. Todd looked around and then broke the silence. "Is that you, Annabelle?" he whispered.

"It could be a bear," mentioned Parker, who then told us all to yell once more.

After all the screaming, there was a moment of silence. The loud sound of breaking branches was coming from the surrounding woods. This time, it was much closer. The sound grew louder as it approached, and then it began to thrash back and forth in the bushes. The noise grew louder and louder. Then a deep voice began to yell, "I'm going to kill you all!" as a large man burst through the bushes swinging a machete.

Parker jumped to his feet and made a beeline down the path toward the dam. Buck was only a few steps behind him; neither of them turned to look back. Jimmy went the opposite direction, running west because that was the way back to his house. Scooter had already taken refuge behind the tree next to the creek. I was fifteen feet up in the tree while Lexi and Sara were screaming and running not far behind their brother and Buck.

The only one who stayed behind was Todd, too frozen to move. He stood face to face with a tall, muscular man holding a machete in his right hand. The man was wearing an old flannel shirt and blue jeans, and he had on muddy work boots. His camouflage baseball hat tilted down just enough to cover his eyes. The beard and mustache on his face made it impossible for Todd to tell if the man was upset or smiling; he just stood there, not moving an inch. Todd swallowed hard as he took a step backward, but he paused to get a closer look at the man. He proceeded to peddle back one step at a time, trying to put some distance between him and the intruder.

The man began to lower the machete to his side. He took a large step forward. Todd froze at the man's action. I could tell from my spot in the tree that Todd must be wondering where the rest of us were and why we had left him there to die.

I caught a glimpse in the moonlight of Buck and Parker down the path a ways. It looked like they were making their way back to camp. Then I looked north and spotted Jimmy doing the same.

Something inside me snapped, like a light bulb coming on, and I began my descent. The fear had startled me before I realized who it was. I noticed Scooter was still hiding behind the large tree near the water's edge. Waving my hand, I motioned to him to join me. Taking a few steps from behind the tree, we saw Todd standing before the large man towering in front of him.

The two of us walked and stood next to Todd. A look of relief washed over his face as he realized he was no longer alone. He always talked about his days in the big city and strength in numbers. Off in the distance, we could hear Buck, Parker, and Lexi talking as they approached. At the same time, we heard Jimmy coming in the other direction. Everyone seemed to grow visibly more confident as our numbers continued to grow. *Eight against one seemed to be a fair fight.*

"So, you must be Todd," the large man said.

"How do you know my name?" mumbled Todd.

"I'm Mr. Malone, Buck and Johnny's father."

"Oh shit, man. You scared the crap out of me."

Grabbing me by the head with one arm and putting me in a headlock, Todd made a fist and then rubbed his knuckles on the top of my head. "Hertz donut," Todd laughed in relief.

"Uncle, uncle," I cried out as Todd released me from his grip. "So what are you doing out here, Pops?"

Before he could answer, Buck and the girls had made their way back to camp. "Hey, Mr. Malone," Parker yelled as he waved. "What brings you out here tonight? Don't you trust us?"

"I do, but I saw a storm coming your way and wanted to make sure you guys were safe," he answered.

"Dad, we're fine," Buck snarled a bit.

"I trust you boys; you know that," he paused, "but I promised your mother I would check on you. You know how she is." He rolled his eyes. "But when I heard you telling the story, I couldn't resist." He laughed as he turned to leave.

We all shook our heads in agreement. Buck even commented, "Nice, real nice to pick on a bunch of kids."

"Well, have fun. I guess we'll see you sometime tomorrow," he mentioned as he walked away.

The camp was silent for a few minutes. Buck and Parker walked a little ways down the path to make sure he was gone. Once there was no sign or sound of him, they returned to camp. Everyone enjoyed a good laugh. It didn't take long before the girls took off and headed home, too. After all of that excitement, the six of us sat around the fire sharing a few more marshmallows, and the older boys tried another cigarette.

"Time to hit the sack, boys," said Parker as he crawled to his tent.

"Goodnight, Johnny-boy," Buck yelled from his tent. The others followed suit. It almost sounded like the ending of a popular television show. Everyone giggled, except me, I finally laid my head down and quickly fell asleep.

Chapter Five

"Now boys, strange things happen at night, and after that big scare we had, I was out like a light. Not all of the boys slept as soundly as I did, especially Jimmy. He told me later what happened to him that night, so I'm gonna try to remember it just like he told me."

* * *

After a few hours of sleep, Jimmy grew restless. Unable to sleep, he tossed and turned in his tent. Something weighed heavy on his mind. He wanted to share it with the rest of us, but deep down, he knew we wouldn't believe him.

Crawling out of his sleeping bag, he reached over to unzip his tent. Making his way outside, he stood in the cool, crisp morning air and took a deep breath. A calm, quiet, peaceful feeling settled over him as he looked around. He stretched his arms outward and arched his back. *Aw, that felt good,* he thought to himself as he listened to his back crack.

The light of the moon penetrated through the trees, casting just enough light for him to see the fog rise from the cool creek water. The red-hot glow from the fire was all that remained in the pit. He walked over, picked up a few logs, and laid them on the fire. It wouldn't be long until they would ignite. He smiled at the sound of loud snoring that resonated from inside Parker's tent.

Turning, he ventured cautiously away from camp, stopping about thirty yards in the woods. He had a sudden urge to go, and standing behind a tree, he relieved himself. Tilting his head back, he closed his eyes. "Aaaah," he moaned and smiled. Then a strange feeling rocked his body. He could sense something was wrong. It was too quiet; not even the sound of crickets was present.

He opened his eyes, briefly looked around, a nervous feeling settled over him when he noticed a woman wearing an old white housedress standing some twenty feet away. Panicked, he tried to zip his fly as quickly as possible, but he caught it on his pants, stuck. He fought with his trousers until it finally jerked free.

When he got up the nerve, he poked his head around to see if she was still there; she was. His eyes blinked several times, his mouth hung open, unable to speak. She looked to be in her mid-to-late twenties and had beautiful long hair cascading down her back. She was gorgeous. She glanced in his direction. Jimmy pulled back, unsure what to do next. He paused to think before slowly poking his head around again to see if she was still there. Her face appeared only a foot away from his, and she winked at him.

Startled, he ducked behind the tree. *How did she get over here so quickly?* He wondered. He stood for a moment as trembling waves passed through his body. Then, slowly looking around the corner again, he gazed directly into her loving eyes. Her pale skin glowed. She smiled at him, and he smiled back. Then he noticed the fire burning back at camp. He was stunned; he could see through her transparent body. He fumbled around the tree some more. A cold breeze whipped in the woods. He shivered as the temperature quickly dropped around him. He tried to regain his composure. *She's a ghost.*

This isn't real; I must be dreaming, he repeated in his mind. He moved his hand over his arm and pinched himself, feeling a sharp pain. He pinched himself again to make sure. *I'm not dreaming,* he thought dismally.

He darted a few feet away and took cover behind a larger tree. Taking a deep breath, he looked to the right and sighed in relief. She was gone. He turned to the left, still no one. He was pressing his back to the tree when an ominous feeling engulfed him. She appeared out of nowhere and stood before him. Jimmy was frozen and unable to move; they stared at one another. She seemed to study him from top to bottom.

"What… do you want?" he whispered as the words choked out of his mouth.

"You can see me?" She paused. "Fascinating! Very few can see me." She smiled, and her eyes flashed with amazement.

His lips quivered. "Who… are you? …What… do you want with me?" he stuttered.

"Ah, someone told the story, didn't they?" she hissed.

"It wasn't me. I... swear… it wasn't me."

She raised her hand to his lips and placed a cold finger over his mouth. Jimmy, wide-eyed, did as she asked and remained silent.

"You know who I am, don't you? I'm pretty sure you know what I want," she whispered.

"I… d...d…don't know," he managed to say.

"Ssssh," she suggested, pushing her lips together. "You have something that belongs to me, and I want it back. Do you understand?" She hissed.

"I'm not sure…" Jimmy questioned.

"I'll give you some time to think about it."

"Okay." He looked puzzled.

"Keep it safe. I'll be in touch," she promised and flashed him a dazzling smile. Drifting upward, she dissipated into the trees.

Off in the distance, a hoot owl could be heard followed by another. The sound of crickets chirping rang out as the forest came back to life. Jimmy stood with his back pressed against the tree, too frightened to move. *What happened? Where did she go and what did she think I had that belonged to her?*

Jimmy's head jerked forward, his chin bouncing off his chest. Briefly startled, he woke up and found himself still leaning against the tree. He quickly looked around, his eyes darted to the left and then the right, but no one was in sight. He smiled in relief. Stepping out from behind the large oak, he made his way back to the tent. *I must have been sleepwalking,* he tried to convince himself. *Just another one of those bad dreams.* He snuggled back into his sleeping bag and drifted off the minute his head hit the pillow.

* * *

Morning came quickly. I was the first to wake. Unzipping my tent. I crawled out, and the cool, crisp, morning air slapped

58

me right in the face. At that point, I hadn't heard Jimmy's story. Soon, the sun would rise from the east, and the morning mist hanging over the creek would be gone. The splashing sound of water caught my attention. I looked up and saw a medium-sized black bear had torn a hole in the top of the wooden crate that housed our morning breakfast. The bear had one of the trout in his mouth and would soon be working on another if I didn't act quickly.

Noticing the fire was almost out, I crawled toward it, keeping as low as possible to go unnoticed. I could tell by the red glow that the coals were still hot, and it wouldn't take much to get the fire going again. I army-crawled my way around the tent, grabbed a few logs from the woodpile, and made my way back the same way. So far I had gone undetected. I laid a few smaller branches onto the hot coals. Cupping my hands around my mouth and pressing my lips together, I began to blow. I blew several times, and each time the coals grew brighter and brighter. Then a small flicker and one of the branches ignited. The flames grew rapidly, and I added another log. I listened to the crackle of the flames grow louder.

The bear was too busy eating to notice what I was doing. I knew if I didn't do something quickly, we wouldn't have anything left for breakfast. I was also concerned that the bear could turn on my friends and me if I didn't act fast. My brain remembered that most wild animals don't like fire. Laying the ends of several long branches in the fire, I tried to make a torch. I picked up two of the longer pieces and stood up. Keeping the flames in front of me, I took a tentative step forward and then another. The bear still hadn't noticed me. He was far too busy enjoying his breakfast. It was now or never.

"Yaaa," I squeaked, I sounded like a little child who had just got in trouble. I guess I was nervous. The bear didn't hear me, and if he had, he didn't feel threatened.

I swallowed and tried again, "Yaaa." This time a little louder, yet still no movement from the bear. *What am I? Some cowboy trying to rustle up cows or move horses, I* thought. *I have to do better than that if I want this bear out of our camp.* I nervously took a few more steps toward the bear. My hands were shaking, I began swinging the fire lit branches back and forth in slow motion. Then in a loud voice, I yelled, "HEY!" Now I had the bear's attention. He turned his big furry head to look at the flames and me standing about ten feet away. I waved the fire back and forth again as I yelled once more.

Not wanting to walk away from his free meal, the bear turned toward me and roared. I trembled, cursing myself that I had made a huge mistake. Frozen and unable to move, I stared into the eyes of the bear. The bear stared back. *Oh, so you want to play chicken?* I held the staring record at school. I once stared at another boy for over twenty minutes without blinking. The other boy blinked and backed down, making me the champion at school. I felt confident that I could win, even if it was a bear. But the bear had other plans, and I realized this was not some silly school contest. No, I was interrupting his meal. The bear stood on his hind legs, standing some six feet tall, and roared at me. I no longer felt confident because this wasn't just a small bear anymore. I quickly took a few steps back.

I could hear the sound of tents unzipping behind me. The cavalry was about to arrive. Scooter was the first to open his tent. Sticking his head out to see what was making all the noise, he noticed the bear. I saw him quickly pull his head back in and zip the tent shut. *Some help he was going to be. Maybe the others will be braver and help me.*

Jimmy poked his head out, noticed the bear, scrambled to his feet, and grabbed a branch from the fire. He yelled and took a few steps forward. Another zipper. This time, Buck came out holding an ax in front of him, the one he had used the night before to cut the firewood. Taking a few steps forward, he stood beside me. Then Parker came out, wearing fluorescent yellow boxer briefs. The sight of those briefs was enough to scare any bear away, especially since the rest of us wore jeans or cut off shorts and t-shirts. But not Parker, nothing but bright yellow boxers. He picked up a branch from the fire and took a stand alongside the rest of us.

Scooter just watched from the safety of his tent. All the noise must have got the better of Todd, and he finally came out to join the rest of us.

The bear roared once again. I think he could tell he was out-numbered, but I'm not sure that it mattered to him. He stood and roared again before coming down on all fours. He turned and poked his head back into the fishing basket. Using his large jaws, he clamped down on another fish, turned, and took a few steps toward the west side of the camp. We watched as he began to trot off with one of our fish dangling from his mouth. What a relief that was to see the bear leaving! I felt a weight lift off my shoulders.

"Oh, man, that was scary," I said, still trembling.

"Are you nuts, man? That was a stupid thing to do," Buck scolded me.

61

"You must have a death wish," Parker yelled. "That was the dumbest thing I have ever seen you do."

"I thought he was pretty brave, taking on the bear and all," Jimmy chimed in.

"Well, you would, and if he would've been hurt or even…" Buck stopped midsentence; all he could do was shake his head. "I would be the one who would have to tell my parents." He turned his back to us.

"Next time something like this happens, you wake us up first. We know how to deal with these types of situations. Do you understand?" snapped Parker.

"Yes," I replied and bowed my head, shame turning my cheeks a light shade of red.

"I think he's a hero," said Scooter. "He saved us all."

"Me too, so you mother hens should back off," Todd blurted out.

"Thanks, man," I called to Todd and Scooter as I walked toward the half-submerged fishing basket. I could see there were still a few fish left. I pulled the cage up, allowing the water to drain, and turned to the others. "We still have breakfast!"

"Good. You clean them, and I'll cook," said Scooter.

I walked a few paces away and found a flat rock that would be perfect for my cleaning station. My nerves were finally settling down. Todd came over to watch, obviously wanting to learn how to gut and clean fish. I pulled the largest one from the basket and held it down on the flat rock. Placing the knife on the fish's head, I sliced it off.

The look on Todd's face said it all, and I really hoped he wasn't going to get sick. I continued to fillet them, handing one piece of meat at a time to him as I finished cleaning each fish. Then I motioned Todd to place the fillets in the frying pan where Scooter was waiting to cook them. Scooter had just put a half stick of butter in when the first piece of fish hit the pan. Oh, the sizzling sound of fish in the frying pan was awesome. The smell filled the air and swept through the camp, making my mouth water. Some of the boys had just returned from their morning potty break while others, like Parker, had finally put on some clothes.

Everyone gathered around the camp as plates of food were handed out. Scooter had become a pretty good cook. "Nothing better than fish and beans for breakfast," Parker said.

"Yeah, well, it's your turn to clean everything up today," I said between mouthfuls of hot, buttery fish.

"Oh, I don't think so," replied Buck.

"As the youngest ones here, it's your duty. I had to do that when I was the youngest," replied Parker. Buck nodded his head in agreement.

Looking at each other, Scooter, Jimmy, and I mulled their statement around in our heads. With a few shrugged shoulders and tilts of our heads, we came to realize Buck and Parker were right. Looking back now, it truly wasn't fair at all. They never were the young ones, just smarter at getting out of the chores, that's all.

"So, what's our plans today?" Todd asked, curiously, stretching his legs and relaxing back on a log. Being his first camping trip, he naturally didn't know what we did all day.

Several options came to mind. Hiking to the top of the mountain was one. There was nothing better than a trip to the top of the mountain because the view was great. And who knew what we would find on an excursion like that. The second option was to go for a trip down the creek. The weather was right for a rafting trip. It was supposed to hit eighty degrees, so the water should feel great. The third option was to fish some more and spend a lazy day around camp. After much discussion, the rafting trip won out. We all knew there would be plenty of time to go fishing when we returned.

* * *

Zack and Daniel looked at one another before turning back to look at me.

"Do you expect us to believe you fought a bear when you were our age?" Zack questioned.

"I didn't fight the bear; I just stood up to him," I replied. "There is a difference." The boys shrugged their shoulders in agreement.

"Did Jimmy see a ghost?" asked Zack.

"That's what he said."

"That must have been cool. Do you think ghosts are real?"

"As far as I know, they are, but I don't want to give away the rest of the story."

"All right then, go ahead and continue," replied Zack.

"It's not like we have anything else to do," Daniel smirked as he sank deeper into the recliner.

"Well, that's groovy," I said to the boys.

"Not cool, Dad, not cool at all." Zack frowned and shook his head.

Daniel giggled. "Just finish your story, Daddy-O."

Chapter Six

Parker scattered the branches around the fire pit. Todd scooped up the shovel and tossed small loads of dirt on the open flames to snuff them out. We all watched as the smoke rolled upward. It was easier to start a new fire than run the risk of letting it burn while we were gone.

Scooter, Jimmy, and I cleaned up the dishes and then began putting our personal belongings inside the tents.

"You just need to wear your shorts and sneakers today. Leave your socks and shirts behind. It's nice having dry socks while your shoes are drying by the fire," said Parker.

"As long as your bright yellow shorts stay covered, then I'm down with that," roared Jimmy.

We busted out laughing; Jimmy's comment had hit a home run. Parker was the only one who seemed a little embarrassed, yet he offered no response. After a long moment of silence, Parker finally asked, "Do we want to cut across the marsh?"

Buck glanced around at the rest of us, trying to get a feel for our thoughts. Scooter lifted up both hands in front of him to signal he had no idea what to do while I only shrugged my shoulders. Of course, Todd didn't know what the best route would be since he was new to the area. That left only Jimmy, and being the group wild man, he was always up for adventure. Jimmy just smiled and shook his head.

"Okay, then it's set; the swamp it is," Parker announced. The swamp was the quickest way to the road, saving us valuable time.

The marshlands were a large swampy area. That was all that remained of the picture perfect lake that once was here. Back in the day, it was mainly used for floating logs downstream to the old ax factory. They say it provided good fishing and swimming on those hot summer days. Since the dam broke, all that remained were the wetlands, a large swamp filled with knee-high water and a few dirt paths. Using it as a short cut was not our best option, especially since snakes, spiders, and other things filled the marsh.

This was our first trip through the swamp this summer. We had no idea what we would find; maybe a muskrat or beaver family had moved in over the winter. The last thing we wanted to do was surprise one of them, especially if they had a fresh litter of pups. They'd chew our legs off defending their babies. But this didn't scare us, not like the reed plants that stood some six to seven feet tall with their razor sharp edges. The fact that we were only wearing shorts made the journey that much more dangerous.

Taking long strides as we ventured into the swamp, Parker and Buck took the lead, closely followed by Todd and Jimmy. Bringing up the rear were Scooter and I. There were many acres of land to cover, most of them filled with cattails. Cattails made the best torches at night, mainly because the tops were a dense brown substance about an inch in diameter. This plant was the best thing to use when we were out in the woods at night. We would often pluck a few just to be on the safe side.

We walked a short distance before coming to the first patch of water. It was only about twenty feet across and contained a few reed plants, but none of us knew how deep the water was. Parker carried a walking stick, which he raised into the air and slowly pushed the end of the stick into the water. It appeared to be only a few inches deep. He stepped into the water and quickly jerked his foot out. "Dang, that water's cold!" he shouted.

After he shook off the cold, Parker slowly stepped back in and then inched in the other foot. Placing the walking stick in the water, followed by another step, he repeated the process, making his way across. "It's easy," he shouted back. The rest of us followed closely behind. We all found ourselves back on dry land. None of us worried about how wet or muddy our sneakers got since we planned to swim in the creek.

As we continued, the marked path narrowed before fading away. Now it was time to rough it. Parker swung the walking stick back and forth in front of him as he made his way through the tall blades of grass. Using his feet, he pressed the tall reeds to the ground, clearing a path for the rest of us through more shallow water followed by more patches of dry land. Soon the reeds were much taller than any of us, making visibility impossible.

Everyone stopped; we needed to make sure we were heading in the right direction. No one wanted to go in circles in the swamp.

"Are we lost?" squawked Jimmy.

"No, we're not lost," Parker barked back. "We're just taking a break."

"We don't need a break. Just admit it; we're lost."

"Dream on, man," Parker spat back. Then he turned to Buck and whispered, in a low voice, but we all heard him ask Buck if he knew which way was out. Buck motioned for me to come over. Parker folded his hands together, I placed my foot in his hands, and he gave me a leg up. I climbed up on Buck's shoulders to look around. As Buck raised me in the air, I could see our house about a hundred yards straight ahead. I wordlessly pointed straight ahead in the direction that we needed to go.

"I told you we're lost," Jimmy said, refusing to let it drop.

Two large crows flew into view, squawking and cawing as they circled above. They drew closer each time they passed. Jimmy let out a yell as they appeared to dive directly at us. He ducked, lost his footing, and fell face first into the mud. I leaned back and swung my hands in front of my face. Then I lost my balance and fell backward off Buck's shoulders, landing flat on my back on a soft patch of muck. It almost knocked the wind out of me. Parker, then Buck, laughed while Todd and Scooter looked a bit puzzled.

The crows flew away and then circled to make another pass, which sent Jimmy back to the ground as the crows made another dive at us. Parker couldn't contain himself and busted out laughing. Jimmy quickly sprang to his feet. This time, he turned and lunged directly at Parker. He fell face first as Parker sidestepped his first attack. The grin on Parker's face seemed to

69

infuriate Jimmy. He jumped to his feet and ran directly at him, this time making contact. He wrapped his arms around Parker's midsection and lifted him into the air before slamming him on his back.

I lay on my back watching the two wrestle around in the muck. The sloshing sounds of mud, along with the grunts and groans, were enough to keep any animals away. The ruckus continued for a few minutes as the rest of us just sat and watched. I guess his frustration had been building up for some time. Jimmy had told me often that he had enough of Parker's lip. Maybe this was good for both of them.

The temperature was pushing eighty degrees. They both looked exhausted, and beads of sweat rolled down their faces. Finally, the wrestling match slowed before coming to a complete stop. Covered in mud, the two of them sat on their butts, exchanging nasty glances as the two crows squawked from a distant tree.

"Are you done?" Parker asked, trying to catch his breath.

"Yeah, sure," Jimmy snarled.

Buck stepped forward, offering a hand to help each of them and pulling them to their feet. "It's not that far," he said calmly, pointing in the direction of our house.

"Why'd you push me?" Jimmy asked.

"I didn't push you," Parker said, surprised by the accusation. "You hit the deck like you were afraid of something.

"It was the crows," I replied.

The others looked at me and then to each other, apparently not sure what to make of my comment. "What crows?" Buck asked.

"The crows that attacked us before Parker pushed me," said Jimmy.

I pointed toward a large spruce where the two birds sat watching. Then I realized they were gone. I guess only Jimmy and I had seen the crows. I found this a bit puzzling; I didn't know what to make of it. *Why hadn't the others seen them? They were huge. How could they miss them?* Many questions raced through my mind, but I decided to keep my mouth shut. I think Jimmy had read my mind, for he didn't say another word.

"Let's get moving," Parker said, shaking his head. I could hear Parker say to Buck, "What's wrong with those two?" as we started in the direction of the house.

"Maybe it's the thing with the bear this morning that freaked 'em out. You know how it is; they're still kids, man," Buck replied shrugging his shoulders.

Jimmy and Parker exchanged a few more glances at each other as we made our way across the last stretch of swampy land. Scooter and Todd brought up the rear, their chuckles echoing up to us. No doubt they were talking about the fight.

In a matter of minutes, the six of us emerged from the swamp. We walked across the backyard. Buck motioned for Parker and Jimmy to step around the side of the house. "If you want to come in the house, you'll have to clean up a bit," Buck told them as he unraveled the green garden hose. Turning the cold water on, he sprayed each of them. Parker yelled in disgust when the cold water pelted him. Jimmy reached his hand out to let them know he could do it himself. I smiled and enjoyed watching Buck hose them down. It didn't take long to clean them up.

Scooter and I went into the basement, opened the freezer, and grabbed some popsicles. One for each of us. "Now this is the life," I said as I went back outside and passed one to Jimmy and one to Todd. We sat in the shade along the side of the house, slurping down the cold multi-colored sticks of joy.

"So what's next?" Todd asked.

"When we finish these," I said, tilting my Popsicle forward, "we head over to the cycle shop."

The cycle shop, as we called it, was a locally owned business that sold lawn mowers, motorcycles, snowmobiles, and anything else that had a small engine mounted on it. It wasn't a big place, but it was the only one in town.

"What's at the cycle shop?" asked Todd.

"That's where we keep our rafts," replied Buck.

The shop tossed all the trash out the back of the building. Not your normal garbage, no, that went into the dumpster like everyone else's. No, the trash I'm talking about was the empty wooden and Styrofoam crates. Motorcycles came packed in nice, big, five-or-six-foot pieces of foam. Most of them were eight to ten inches thick, some even larger. They made the best river rafts for guys our size. Sometimes, we even got lucky and found some old inner tubes that just needed a little patching.

Soon there was nothing left of the popsicles but the sticks that each of us held in our hands.

"Are we ready?" Buck asked, standing up and brushing off the back of his shorts. He handed his leftover stick to me, motioning for me to throw it away. Each of them rose to their feet, passing sticks to me as they walked. I tossed them into the garbage can before placing the silver metal lid back on the top. Walking in pairs, the six of us made our way up a steep twenty-foot embankment to the foot of Lizardville Road. The narrow, two-lane, paved road stretched around the mountain. It would lead us directly to the motorcycle shop.

Parker and Buck walked several feet ahead of our pack. Buck told me later that Parker was still upset and thinking of how he could plot his revenge against Jimmy. But Buck kept insisting for him to drop it, so he changed the subject entirely and asked if Parker was going to get a job over the summer.

He said he had thought about it then told him that Lexi had found a job. She started last week working at that new burger place in Mill Hall. The Burger King, he thought it was called. "And, oh yes, they wear those puffy hats and sing little songs."

Scooter kicked at small pebbles that lay alongside the road. I stared at the gravel in amazement. I watched Scooter pick certain rocks to kick. "Do you hear that?" I yelled, turning my attention behind us to see if a car or truck was coming. Sometimes the old log trucks used this road to get to the sawmill. Of course, it could be a quarry truck, too. They were also loud and rumbled past about twenty times a day.

As luck would have it, neither of them appeared. A car purred around the bend, making its way up the grade, and from the looks of it, the car was an older model Chevy. A '55 Chevy Nomad, *a monster car*, I thought to myself. The sound had everyone's attention as we stopped to look at the approaching vehicle. Some of us sat while others leaned on the guardrails. The sound of the engine grew as the cherry red auto approached. The bright aluminum wheels were mesmerizing, just frozen in time as the car rolled up. Scooter raised his arm in the air, bent at the elbow with his fist balled tightly. He moved it up and down, desperately trying to get the driver to blow the horn.

"What a bitchin ride," Parker said, almost drooling on himself.

"That ride's blazing hot, man. I wish I owned it," Buck responded when he noticed Scooter making his hand motion. "What are you doing, you idiot? That's for trucks! That's so embarrassing." He hung his head as he turned to face Parker. "I don't know why we bring these kids with us all the time."

The horn blared as the hot ride purred past.

"You and me both," said Parker.

"Huh," Scooter responded.

"Ya got lucky this time," Parker said, standing up as he and Buck started down the road. Scooter and I stepped off the guardrail and continued on. Todd and Jimmy followed bringing up the rear. The two of them had been pretty quiet since the scuffle in the swamp.

A few more minutes of walking before Gibbons Cycle Shop came into view. Only one car sat in the parking lot, but not the '55 Nomad we were hoping to see. It was an old '63 Plymouth Belvedere, gray in color and still in mint condition. We recognized the car right away. It belonged to old man Smithers. He was a tall, frail, grumpy old man who was balding. He lived in an old cottage that sat right on the bank of the creek. It used to be a hunting camp that he converted into a home for him and his family. It wasn't too far from the road, just a few miles upstream from where we camped.

Now, we had nothing against him other than the fact that every time we floated by his house he got upset. He'd start yelling and throwing things at us. Once he threw a large, black, plastic spoon covered in spaghetti sauce at us. Chunks of tomato and meat flew off of it before landing in the creek. He could never quite reach us, though. I guess he was getting too old to throw that far. He acted like we were trespassing on his property, but we weren't; the creek wasn't private property. Nobody owned the water.

When we floated past his house, we always stayed as quiet as possible and hugged the base of the giant rock wall that reached the sky. The jagged rocks went straight up some forty feet. At the top, they gently sloped into the mountains. There were two ways to get to the top of the wall—one was to climb the rocks, but if you fell, it was almost certain death. The water was only a few feet deep at the base, not deep enough to stop you from hitting the bottom. The other way was to hike up the other side of the mountain and go over the top and down this side until you reached the top of the cliffs that overlooked his property.

Old man Smithers didn't want anyone near his house. They say he used to be a nice guy when he was younger, but everything changed after his wife and son passed away. Something he never quite got over. A young male driver from Mill Hall had caused the accident. He'd only had his driver's license a few months, and to top it off, the police report said the young man had been drinking. Maybe that's why he didn't want any young boys near his house; maybe they reminded him of that tragic day.

Nevertheless, he wasn't going to keep us off the water this fine summer day. Trying to be as quiet as possible, we went around the back of the cycle shop. No one wanted a confrontation with old man Smithers. We just wanted to borrow some large Styrofoam crates and get on our way.

The backside of the shop sloped downward into the woods. It was an old dumping ground; the township had been after them for years to clean up the garbage. To us, this wasn't mess; it was a goldmine. Sometimes, we found a soda bottle or two. That's when we had the time to rummage through the trash. Today, we wanted to be quick and pick out six sturdy rafts that would carry us on our mission, and we were in luck. There were a lot of new Styrofoam pieces lying around. They must have had a new shipment arrive recently.

"Dudes, look at all the nice rafts," said Parker.

"You got that right," replied Buck.

We rummaged through the larger pieces of Styrofoam. Scooter pulled out a nice piece about ten inches thick, maybe three feet wide, and almost six feet long. I found the other half to the one Scooter had. After realizing that Scooter and I were done, I turned my attention to Todd, who wasn't sure what to look for in a raft. I pointed out a few things that I thought would make a good raft.

"You're looking for a nice thick piece, one that doesn't have too many cut-outs. Places where the tires, seats, or engine were carved out, that's the thin areas, and they will break when you're on the water. You also need to make sure you have a nice area for your butt," I explained as I pointed these areas out on the large piece of foam that Todd was holding.

Todd quickly tossed that piece aside before picking up a real nice one.

"That would make a great raft," I said as I pointed at the large thick foam board Todd had just picked up.

"Found mine," proclaimed Jimmy.

"It looks a little weak in the middle," Buck pointed out.

"Its fine," Jimmy snapped.

"Just trying to keep you dry," replied Buck in a calm voice.

"If I need your advice, I'll ask, got it?" Jimmy hissed.

"Don't be a chump," said Parker. "He's only trying to help."

"Don't bother," barked Jimmy in a nasty tone.

"Whatever," replied Parker as he rolled his eyes.

I hoped these two were not going to fight all day. After all, this was supposed to be a fun day. The six of us tucked our makeshift rafts under our arms. One by one, we crept toward the back wall of the shop and then carefully snuck to the far side of the building before stopping. Parker peered around the corner and signaled to us that the coast was clear. We took off in pairs, running at a half trot, and continued north until the shop was no longer in view. The Styrofoam made a weird sound as we ran, like the sound vinyl pants would make rubbing between one's thighs.

Chapter Seven

We continued our journey, trekking down the road in pairs for the next few miles. Parker and Buck kept to themselves as they walked ahead. Not far behind were Todd and Wildman Jimmy, who still looked upset over the fight in the swamp. Enjoying the sun beating down on our backs, Scooter and I brought up the rear.

Lizardville Road curved its way through the small town of Salona. The creek hugged the base of the mountain. By walking on the road, we stayed on a straight path to where we would launch our rafts. We caught glimpses of the creek, which crisscrossed back and forth, resembling a large snake from an aerial view. But the route we were taking would save us time and bring us out five or six miles north of our campsite.

Salona was about the same size as Lizardville, so there wasn't much there. A few homes, a volunteer fire station, and a family-owned general store. The store sold almost anything you were looking for, including gasoline. Mr. Evans always sat behind the counter. The store had been in his family for years. We pooled our money together, trying to raise enough for a soda or two, but we could only muster up forty-seven cents.

Parker and Buck had upset him the last time they were in his store. Parker said he distracted him while Buck stole two candy bars that were located in a box on the counter. Mr. Evans always kept the new candy on the top of the counter. He wanted to make sure all of us kids noticed them.

For some reason, the others appointed me to go to the store. I hesitated, thinking Mr. Evans would recognize me because I looked so much like Buck, but I took the money and traipsed toward the front of the store. The guys carried my raft and waited for me in the back of the building. We all knew there wasn't much I could buy with forty-seven cents, maybe two sodas and a few pieces of penny bubblegum. I knew the guys were hoping for a little more than that, maybe a bag of potato chips to share between us.

I stopped at the corner of the building and poked my head around to get a better look through the large window. I could see there was no one else in the store. *Great timing.* Turning the corner, I nervously walked to the front door. Stepping over the long black rubber hose that stretched across the driveway reaching to a set of gas pumps, I wanted to jump up and down on the rubber hose to make the bell ring inside the store like I had done many times in the past. A feeling deep inside told me that would not be a smart move today since I wanted to ask Mr. Evans for a favor.

I pushed the door open to the clanging of bells that hung over the front door. Mr. Evans emerged from the back room to see who had entered his fine establishment. He was a middle-aged man, your average size. He always wore blue jeans with the cuffs rolled up at the bottom that barely covered his black work boots. Today he wore a plaid flannel shirt that reminded me of a lumberjack who had just come out of the woods, minus the ax.

"Well hello there, young lad," he said in his deep muscular voice.

"Hello," I mumbled and looked away, making sure not to make eye contact.

"Aren't you one of the Malone boys?" asked Mr. Evans as he studied my face with his shifty eyes.

"Ah, yes sir, I am," I nervously replied.

"You have a brother, oh, what's his name?" Mr. Evans tried to remember.

I walked over to the big white cooler box that sat on the floor on the far side of the store. Slowly opening the lid, I reached in and grabbed three Pepsi bottles. Knowing I didn't have enough to pay for them, I closed the lid and made my way back to the counter.

A strange smell hung in the air, not your normal store smell. It smelled like incense, and it made my nose twitch. The store always had this sweet intoxicating smell. Maybe it was the candles he stocked for the ladies or the candy smell that filled the air. Today's smell was different, and I don't know why, but I didn't ask any questions. I just wanted to get the sodas and get out. I placed the sodas on the counter looking up at Mr. Evans, when the clang, clang of the gas pump bells rang out.

"Excuse me a minute, young fellow. I'll be right back," he said as he made his way from behind the counter and exited the front door. Someone had pulled up to the gas pump, and Mr. Evans went out to pump the gas and clean his windshield. I knew if I wanted to take a candy bar or two, now was the time. A feeling deep down inside came rising up in my throat, almost gagging me. I knew it was wrong, and I became a little light headed and unsure of what to do.

I glanced at the gas pumps as I tried to get a better look out the dirty storefront window to see how much time I had before Mr. Evans would return. I became frantic when I spotted old man Smithers' car. He was talking with Mr. Evans, chuckling and laughing as if they were best of friends.

Mr. Evans continued to pump gas. *Oh, this was not good. What if he came in the store?* Panic set in, and I needed an escape plan. I stepped behind the counter and into the back room where the smell of the incense made my eyes water. I tried looking for a window to crawl out. I was in luck. There was a small window about six feet off the ground, just out of my reach. I needed something to stand on, but what, I wondered as I looked around the room.

I spotted the chair behind Mr. Evans' desk. *Perfect,* I thought, I grabbed the chair and starting pulling it toward the window when I noticed the large stacks of money sitting on his desk. *Oh, my,* ones, fives, even a few tens, and a lot of coins, all stacked in small neat piles. Pennies, nickels, dimes, even quarters. My first instinct was to grab a handful and go out the window, but something told me to stop. As I reached to grab the money, I stopped again. There was that feeling. A warm fuzzy feeling deep inside that told me this was wrong. *Don't take things that don't belong to you,* my father always told me.

But it was too easy. It was right there for the taking; I reached again. Clang, clang, it was the bells over the front door. Mr. Evans returned, or maybe both of them had entered the store. I froze. I just couldn't find the strength to move, not even one step. It felt like my legs weighed a hundred pounds each. Thud, thud, thud, the footsteps grew louder—the ringing of the cash register. I could hear the cash door slide open. Mr. Evans was making change for old man Smithers.

How would I explain this if Mr. Evans caught me in the back room? This place was off limits; the sign on the door said, "Employees Only." So many horrible thoughts raced through my mind. *Would he shoot me, hang me from a tree out back, cut me into a million pieces so no one would ever find me?* I needed to move but I couldn't, and when I heard the cash register door close followed by a few more footsteps and the clang of the bells over the door, I knew this was my only chance. I took one step, then another and slowly made my way back to the office door. I pushed it open and peeked around the store. The coast was clear. I stepped out and walked a few feet over to the comic books, took a deep breath, and sat on the floor grabbing a new copy of Superman. A good feeling came over me. I was glad I didn't take the money. I smiled and turned the pages of the comic book. I heard the clang, clang of the bells again.

"Hey boy, you don't read the books unless you intend to buy them," Mr. Evans barked.

"I'm, I'm sorry," I whispered as I folded the book and placed it back on the shelf.

"Was there something you wanted, young man?"

"Ah, just these three sodas."

"That will be sixty cents," he smiled.

"I, I only have forty-seven cents," I sheepishly replied with my head bowed.

"That's fine; I can put the thirteen cents on your old man's tab."

"That would be fine if you can do that. Thanks, Mr. Evans," I replied with a wry smile as I turned and walked toward the front door.

"Hey, wait a minute," he yelled from behind the counter. "When I came back in here a few minutes ago, where were you, boy?"

A nauseous feeling sank deep inside me. Father had always told me three things: *Respect your elders, never steal, and most of all, don't lie. A man's word is all he has in life, and if you lie, your word isn't worth a pile of beans.* I knew right away what I had to do.

"I was sitting over there reading the comic book," I lied and pointed toward the bookrack.

"Okay then, maybe I missed you; you're a small fellow," he reasoned with himself. "Well then, have a good day, and oh, by the way, tell Buck the next time I see him, I expect him to pay for those candy bars he stole."

I glanced up, amazed that Mr. Evans knew Buck took the candy bars. I noticed Mr. Evans eyes had turned pitch black. An evil grin shot across his face, briefly staring at me, and then he began to laugh. He looked possessed.

Fear raced through me. Totally frightened, I scurried toward the door, slamming it open as I bolted through. I couldn't wait to get out of there. I had almost forgotten all about the sodas but grabbed them at the last second. Mr. Evans' face would haunt me the rest of the day; pure evil filled those black eyes.

"Caw, Caw," a large crow called as I ran out of the store. I jumped back, startled by the crow that sat just above the entrance door. I stumbled a bit and almost dropped the bottles. I backed up into the wall. I was shocked when I noticed more crows perched on top the power line to my left, and several more sat in the surrounding trees. Twenty, maybe thirty in all. I had never seen that many crows in one place before. *How on earth did that one crow get so big? It was the size of a large dog.*

Quickly, I shuffled my feet sideways, while pushing my body to the corner of the building. Then I made a beeline to the back of the store. I could hear the crows squawking as I ran. Turning the corner, I tried to catch my breath. I bent over, put the bottles on the ground, and placed my hands on my knees, I was gasping for air. You would think I'd just run a marathon. Was it the crows or that look on Mr. Evans face that sent shivers up my spine?

The others looked at me a little bewildered. "That's all you got, three soda pops?" Buck yelled.

"One for me and one for you, Buck," Parker exclaimed as he tried to grab two bottles.

"I don't think so," I snapped. "Not this time, and oh, by the way, Buck, Mr. Evans wants his candy bars back." I glared at Buck and Parker, grabbed the soda and handed one bottle to Scooter and the other to Jimmy.

Buck and Parker were stunned, speechless for the first time all day. I had never stood up to Buck like that. I think I caught them both off guard. I popped the top on the soda bottle by using my belt buckle; the sound fizzed in my ears. Raising the bottle to my lips, I took a long deep gulp before passing it to Todd. Scooter did the same and then reluctantly handed his to Buck. Jimmy held the soda as long as he could before finally giving it to Parker, who gave a friendly nod to say thank you.

"You guys should have seen Mr. Evans' eyes. They were black as night. Pure evil, sinister if you want to know the truth," I told them, still trembling. "I've never seen anything like 'em, those eyes, those black eyes. I mean something was different about him today."

"I think your imagination is getting the best of you," said Todd.

"No, that was not Mr. Evans. At least, not the Mr. Evans I know," I repeated, my voice rising as I spoke. "Plus, you should have seen all the crows out front. They just watched me with their beady eyes; I think they wanted to kill me."

"What crows?" Buck asked, a little bewildered when he looked toward the front of the store.

"Enough," barked Jimmy. "Are we gonna hit the creek or not?"

I was a little surprised that Jimmy was ready to move on and not even listen to my story. We stood looking at each other for a few moments, bobbed our heads, shifting our feet side to side, even grumbled a bit. I don't think anyone believed me. I stashed the bottles under some brush. *I'll return them later, I* thought. We picked up our Styrofoam rafts and walked toward the road. Like always, Buck and Parker took the lead. "What crows?" Parker snickered as he shook his head, making it no secret that he did not believe me.

Scooter walked alongside Todd in the middle. I brought up the rear with Wildman Jimmy, who had motioned for me to walk with him.

Jimmy turned to me and whispered, "I need to tell you something, man, and please don't think I'm crazy." My eyes stayed glued on Jimmy. "I'm not crazy. My parents think I'm nuts, but I'm not. I know what you mean about Mr. Evans. I've seen it before. Those black eyes, that blank stare that leads to nowhere. He's possessed; I know it," Jimmy's eyes widened as he looked around.

Nodding in approval, I gave Jimmy my full attention. He went on to explain. "The stories about Annabelle are true. They say Annabelle had a daughter. After her mother's disappearance, the child went to a foster home for a while before finally moving in with her aunt.

"The daughter's name was Elizabeth. She grew up and stayed in the local area. Elizabeth eventually got married and had a daughter of her own. The girl was born sometime around nineteen-twenty. She named her daughter after her mother, but they called her Anna." He paused and rubbed his hand over his mouth. "I was told Anna lived on the other side of the mountain in a town called Sugar Valley. When she got older, she met and married a nice businessman whose name was Tom Evans."

Surprised, this name caught me off guard.

"What do you mean Evans? You mean the same Mr. Evans that runs the general store?"

"Not quite, in the forties, Anna and Tom had a son. They named him after his father. Tom Evans, Jr. After he had graduated high school, he moved back to this side of the mountain and opened this general store. Yes, the very same person that owns the store today."

"No way," I breathed, feeling the hairs on the nape of my neck begin to stand.

"Oh yes, the very same one. It's in his blood," Jimmy said.

"What's in his blood?" I asked.

"Some of the old stories say that Annabelle was into witchcraft. Spells and all that jazz, spooky stuff, if you know what I mean," Jimmy explained.

Goose bumps raced up my arms.

"You're freaking me out, man. Why are you telling me this?" I asked, nervous and a bit confused.

"I needed to tell someone. I tried to tell my parents, but they thought I had lost my mind. My dad says they need to ship me off to a boarding school or something. He says I need to get away from this place because it's making me crazy. But after what you saw today, I knew I could confide in you," he sighed.

"Why should I believe you? You could be making this shit up," I countered.

"But I'm not," exhausted Jimmy.

"Prove it," I demanded.

That's when Jimmy filled me in on his story. About a year ago, Jimmy had gone to the general store to get some candy. As he entered, he realized the place was empty. He then heard a faint sound coming from behind the closed door that led to the back room. *Mr. Evans must be back there,* he thought. Mr. Evans was so consumed in whatever he was doing that he never heard Jimmy enter the store. He was chanting something, a bunch of mumble jumbo to himself. Jimmy walked across the room, following the sounds, and pushing the door slightly open.

He stood in the crack of the doorway, watching Mr. Evans from a distance. The fragrance of incense, a bouquet of wines and spirits, filled the room. The scent was so strong that at first it burned Jimmy's nose to the point where his eyes almost watered. Pinching his fingers over his nose, he prevented that from happening.

The black shades were drawn down covering the window, making the room very dark. Flickering lights from the candles cast shadows on the walls. Mr. Evans was almost dancing, weaving right, then left, and occasionally waving his arms around as he blankly stared into some old black metal pot that sat in the middle of his desk.

Jimmy stood paralyzed, unable to move. The sight was captivating. Like witchcraft, voodoo, or something ancient, he wasn't sure. There was this strange sensation pulling on his entire body, almost like being sucked into a vacuum. Fifteen or twenty minutes passed. He stood frozen in time when Mr. Evans noticed him standing in the doorway.

When he realized Mr. Evans had spotted him, Jimmy stepped back, and the door closed. His eyes popped, his head began to spin, his knees felt weak, and he was unable to move. He tried to take another step back, he tried to run, but he was confused. His legs wouldn't move, he stumbled backward, tripping and landing firmly on his butt. Sitting in the middle of the hardwood floor, he tried to do the crab crawl to escape. Then he tried to scamper backward, but nothing was working. Oh, how he wished he had paid more attention in Biff's gym class.

Mr. Evans quietly watched from the doorway as Jimmy tried to get away. Jimmy's head snapped in the direction of the front door when he heard the latch click, which was strange because no one was over there. A creaking sound from the hinges squeaked as Mr. Evans slowly pushed the office door open. Now standing over Jimmy was the tall, thin man who brought real fear to Jimmy's heart. He wanted to scream yet couldn't. His eyes were bulging out of his head as he stared at Mr. Evans.

Mr. Evans knelt down and with an outstretched hand offered to help Jimmy to his feet, but Jimmy declined.

"Are you okay?" he asked.

"Ah, I don't know. What were you doing in there?" asked Jimmy, continuing to push away.

"Please let me explain. It's something that has been in our family for longer than I can remember. It's a form of meditation."

"That wasn't meditation; I'm not stupid," Jimmy cried out.

"Please, call me Tom."

"I'm not calling you anything, except maybe crazy," Jimmy bellowed, scared and confused, still unable to get up and run.

"Let's face it, Jimmy, no one will ever believe a little hoodlum like you, now, will they?" snarled Tom.

Jimmy frowned; he knew at that moment that Mr. Evans— okay Tom— was right. He had played too many tricks around this town and had a reputation for being a rotten kid. He remembered when he went to the lumber yard, stole some of the workers boots, tied the shoe strings together, and tossed them over the power lines. Then there was another time at the volunteer firehouse; it was bingo night, and he snuck in and took a few numbers out of the bingo jar, numbers B-6 and I-20. Tom was right. No one was going to believe him now. He sank to the floor and placed his hands over his face.

"It's okay. Let me help you up, and I'll explain everything," said Tom.

Jimmy slowly removed his hands from his face and looked up at Tom. He hesitated, then stretched out his hand, took a hold of Tom's, and allowed him to help him to his feet.

Chapter Eight

Tom pulled out a chair and offered it to him, which Jimmy was glad to accept. Then he pulled a nice cold bottle of Pepsi from the cooler. Jimmy's mouth suddenly dried up. He felt like he had been in the Mojave Desert for a month. He noticed the sweat beads dripping down the side of the bottle. *Pop, hiss* the sounds rang out as Tom popped the top from the bottle and handed it to Jimmy.

He took the bottle reluctantly, raised it to his lips, and began to gulp it down. He heard Tom telling him to slow down before he gave himself a headache. Jimmy saw his lips moving, but it seemed like Tom was a thousand miles away. Then the thought struck him, *had he put something in the soda?* Panic rushed through him. Then he tucked his head between his knees, trying not to hyperventilate.

Tom walked to the front windows of the store and pulled down the shades and turned the *closed* sign around. Walking back behind the counter, he pulled another chair out and placed it beside Jimmy. He laid the palm of his hand on Jimmy's back and began to move it in slow circles trying to comfort the young man. Jimmy's breathing began to slow as Tom once again asked him if he was okay.

Jimmy took a few deep breaths trying to control his breathing. *Get a grip*, he repeated to himself over and over in his head. *What's wrong with you?* The thought raced through his mind as his breathing slowly returned to a steady pace.

Jimmy sat up in the chair and looked around. "Sorry about that. I guess I should be going now," he said, trying to stand.

"Relax, I think we need to talk," Tom calmly replied and told him to sit.

"Nothing to talk about, we're good," Jimmy said as he once again tried to stand.

Tom reached out and put a hand on his shoulder, forcing Jimmy back into the chair. "I said we need to talk."

Jimmy felt a lump form in his throat when he tried to swallow. Tom leaned forward. "Can I get you another soda, or a bag of chips perhaps?"

Jimmy shook his head while Tom began to explain. He was only doing an old ritual, something that had been passed down through his family. The best way to describe it was a séance, trying to reach out and talk with loved ones from beyond. Jimmy looked confused.

"I know, you're thinking, 'shouldn't there be a lot of people present for a séance?' Normally yes, but not this one; this one was private. I was trying to communicate with my grandmother and wasn't having any luck. Like always," he paused to think. "Hey, maybe you could help." Tom seemed excited to have someone to help.

Jimmy continued to explain all of this to me as we continued down the road to Big Fishing Creek. We were both looking forward to cooling off in the water.

"So what happened next?" I asked.

Jimmy had stayed with Tom in the store for over an hour. Tom explained to him what he was trying to do, and they even tried it once together, with no luck. Jimmy was beginning to think Tom was a bit of a nut job. However, that opinion changed in one weird moment.

Tom invited Jimmy to work at the store. He would pay him five dollars a week to sweep floors and take out the trash after school. That was a dollar a day, an awful lot of money for a fourteen- year-old in the seventies.

He worked with Tom for several months. Then one day after school, Jimmy came into the store, and Tom looked at him with a blank stare. His eyes were almost black like he was looking into space, a void of some sort. Never saying a word, Tom pulled the shades down and hung the *closed* sign in the window. Then he motioned for Jimmy to follow him into the back room. He carefully stepped into the room and closed the door after Jimmy entered.

"Sometimes, I feel like the séances work and other times they don't. Today I feel like my body has been taken over by someone else." His eyes glazed over, "It feels like I'm only watching. Does this make sense?"

Jimmy mumbled that he understood, but actually, it made sense to explain the black eyes.

"I have something for you," Tom said as he went to his desk. Slowly, he pulled open a drawer and took out a small wooden box with strange carvings on the top and sides. Jimmy couldn't make out what they were since the box was still in Tom's hand. But he was very curious what the box contained.

Tom turned the box over several times in his hand before laying it in the center of the table and instructing Jimmy not to touch it. He said it had been in his family for almost eighty years. It was an old puzzle box, and it contained all of his family secrets, even some spells.

"I was told the box had strange magical powers. But I've yet to figure out how to open it and unlock its true meaning or even know its purpose," he sighed.

Jimmy told me his eyes lit up brighter than a Christmas tree. He was interested in the box and not just because it looked cool. No, Jimmy was interested because it was magical, or at least that's what Tom wanted him to believe.

Jimmy gladly accepted the puzzle box, which seemed to please Tom very much.

"I must warn you there are three rules that you must follow. Number one: never tell anyone about the box, especially your parents. Number two: only you can touch the box. If you let another person touch it, the powers will pass to them. Last, never open the box unless you're alone. That's if you can figure out how to open the box."

Jimmy shook his head and smiled. The box looked so freaking cool. He couldn't wait to get home and try to open it.

Tom pulled out a small purple hand towel and wrapped the box tightly. Then he placed the towel in a cardboard box. Before placing that box into a brown paper bag and handing it off to Jimmy, Tom looked at Jimmy and warned, "It's yours now. Please take good care of it. Protect it with your life."

"I will," Jimmy said with a larger than life smile. He wondered if all of this was just some fairytale story, or did the puzzle box contain magic?

"Do you still have the box?" I blurted.

"I sure do," said Jimmy. "I keep it in the back of my closet."

"I want to see this box. I'm pretty good with puzzle's you know."

"When we get back from this weekend trip, just pop on over, and I'll show it to you," said Jimmy.

"Cool, I can't wait to see this box." I beamed, excited about the possibilities.

* * *

"So, what was in the box?" Zack asked me.

"I think you're feeding us a bunch of garbage," Daniel responded before his dad even had a chance to speak.

Smiling, I said, "I wouldn't feed you a bunch of crap."

"Seriously?" the boys said at the same time and then chuckled.

"Yes, I would only tell you the truth. You know how I feel about lying." I gave them my serious look.

"Please continue," Zack said as he stretched out on the living room couch and stuffed a pillow behind his head.

Chapter Nine

We continued our journey down Lizardville Road. From time to time, a car passed and forced us to the side of the road. Up ahead on the right was the Old Lizardville Cemetery. The graveyard contained headstones dating back to the early eighteen hundreds. They hadn't held a burial there in over fifty years. I never played there because my parents told me the place was haunted. It seemed a little creepy and gave me a weird vibe, so I obeyed and stayed clear of it. I went past many times, on foot or bicycle, but I always stayed on the street side of the fence. The cemetery had become a favorite spot at Halloween. Many of the city folk visited it, and guides offered grave tours. How weird was that? All in hopes of seeing a ghost. I'm sure they left disappointed.

Today was spooky or a little weird. Something in the graveyard caught Jimmy's attention, and he stopped to look at one of the large tombstones. I paused while Jimmy's eyes scoured the grounds.

"See something?"

"Nothing," Jimmy nodded. "I thought I saw…" He paused for a moment, slightly shaking his head. "That can't be." Then he asked, "Do you see anything?" He pointed toward the back of the cemetery in the direction of one of the headstones.

I looked left and then right, searching to find something. "Sorry, man. I don't see anything." I wished I had spotted something, anything, just to reassure Jimmy he wasn't losing it.

Jimmy started talking, and I knew right away he wasn't talking to me. I watched him, then looked at the others as they walked further down the road.

"What do you want with me?" he spoke.

I glanced at Jimmy and then looked around in all directions, nothing but an empty graveyard.

"Who are you talking to?"

"She's here," he whispered.

"Who's here?" I glanced around, trying to figure out who she was.

"Annabelle. She's standing right here." I could hear the frustration in Jimmy's voice, probably because I couldn't see Annabelle.

Jimmy looked puzzled. "Leave me alone," he shouted as he threw his hands up to cover his head and dropping the Styrofoam raft.

"It's all right," I said. I dashed over and grabbed him by the shoulders. Near him, the air was cold, maybe a twenty-degree difference from where I stood a moment ago. I quickly pulled him back toward the road. "Let's get out of here." The two of us picked up the Styrofoam floats and started jogging to catch up with the others. I turned my head a few times to make sure nothing, or no one, was following us. Each time I glanced, I saw nothing. The heat quickly returned. That struck me as odd.

Several minutes passed before Jimmy spoke again. "I'm not losing my mind! She was standing there just like this morning.

She spoke to me, saying, 'You can see me?' I think she was just as surprised as I was. Then she vanished, disappeared. I know this may sound ridiculous, but I swear to you Johnny, I see things. I think… ah, man…" He took in a shaking breath and looked at me. "I think I see ghosts." Desperation laced his voice, and his hands shook with the realization.

I wasn't sure what to believe. Jimmy had told me so many stories that afternoon. I quickly decided to avoid any confrontation and give Jimmy the benefit of the doubt. After all, we had been friends forever, and Jimmy had never lied to me in the past. "It's okay, I believe you."

"Really?"

"Yes."

"Thanks," was the only word that came out of his mouth. Then he turned and began to jog faster so we could catch up to the others. Picking up my pace, I followed closely behind. I couldn't explain the cold feeling that rushed over me when I pulled Jimmy away from the fence. That and the pitch black stare of Mr. Evans' eyes would haunt me that night.

In a matter of minutes, the bridge where we launch our rafts came into view. Of course, Buck and Parker were the first to arrive. I could hear their excited whoops and hollers as they ran onto the bridge. I saw them quickly reach the other side before they leaped over the guard rails and descended the steep incline to the water's edge. Todd and Scooter were the next to arrive and followed the older boys, and shortly after, we joined them.

Jimmy reached out, grabbing my arm to hold me back. "Hey, what I told you back there… let's keep that between us, okay?"

"No problem."

"Pinky swear!" Jimmy said as he extended his finger.

I reached out and locked my finger around his and swore the story about Mr. Evans and Annabelle was our little secret.

"Are you two girls coming?" Parker yelled from under the bridge.

We shared a grin and then hurdled the guard rails. I skidded down feet first, kicking up gravel that covered the embankment, hooting and hollering all the way down.

"Geronimo!" Jimmy yelled as he followed in my skid marks to the bottom, sending many of the stones cascading into the water.

"Who's first?" Todd asked.

We all sat around the base of the bridge, tightening up our shoelaces to make sure they stayed on our feet. The water was calm and crystal clear. We could see all the way to the bottom, some six or seven feet. The creek stretched about fifty feet wide at the base of the bridge. Parker explained a few things about the creek to Todd since he had never been on the creek before. The rest of us had been down this path before, so Parker didn't see the need to explain anything to us. He pointed out how calm the water was here and told Todd we would float for a while before coming to any rapids. Most of them were not that bad, and there was nothing to worry about as long as he followed Buck or himself. His face lit with excitement, Todd nodded and said he was ready to try this.

Parker placed a foot in the water. "Burr," he yelled and then placed his knee on the Styrofoam raft. With a foot in the water, he pushed off toward the center of the creek, trying to find his center of balance. Buck was the next one to launch, but he straddled his raft with both of his feet dragging in the water. Scooter followed doing the same as Buck had done, one foot hanging over each side as he sat in the middle of his raft.

"You're next, Todd," I said pointing to the creek. Todd braced himself for the shock of the cold mountain water. Placing one shoe in the stream, I heard him murmur, "It's not *that* bad." He put the other foot in and took another step before he lunged forward, landing on his belly in the middle of the raft. His arms dangling over the sides, feet hanging off the back, and using his hands to stroke the water, he paddled to the middle of the stream. From the look on Todd's face, I could tell he was very excited.

Jimmy decided to show off a little. There was nothing new about that. After all, we didn't call him the Wildman for nothing. He placed his raft in the water, turned around backward, and straddled the foam before sitting down in the middle. He laid back on the raft and pushed off from the shore. He placed an arm on each side and took a few strokes to move himself to the middle.

I stepped into the water with both feet before placing my raft down. Then deciding to do as Todd had done, I laid on my belly and enjoyed the warm summer sun beating down on my back as I pushed off to join the others.

Carried along by the slow-flowing current, six Styrofoam rafts drifted under the bridge. At this rate, it would take several hours before we reached our camp. Some of us gazed into the glistening water as we watched a large school of fish. That's why it was called Big Fishing Creek. There was plenty of fish, turtles, and other wildlife all set in a peaceful, relaxing environment. *Life doesn't get any better than this,* I thought to myself.

Fifteen minutes had passed. We could still see the bridge standing a few hundred yards to the rear. As we approached the first curve in the creek, nothing but the woods surrounded us. We were isolated and alone. The birds sang in the trees, and the forest sounded alive as we quietly floated past on the peaceful river.

Scooter started telling the others about a time when he and I had left school early, picked up some rafts, and got on the creek still in our school clothes. We were told not to get into the water, but like many boys our age, we didn't listen. After all, what could go wrong? We had been floating for a little while and decided to pull out.

Scooter's enthusiasm grew, and I just sat shaking my head. Telling this story seemed to make Scooter happy. Except for Todd, we'd all heard it before.

There was a large branch that stuck out over the water. The trick was to grab a hold of it as we floated by, then use the branch to pull yourself toward the shoreline, just like using a rope. Scooter explained that as I was coming close to it, instead of me grabbing the branch, it caught me square in the chest, knocking me into the water.

The water was really cold that day, but that wasn't the issue. The real issue was that my mother was going to kill me because I was drenched from head to toe. And I had to be home in twenty minutes. I knew right away I was in serious trouble.

"So what'd he do?" Todd interrupted, asking Scooter while shooting a look at me.

"He did the only thing he could do. He went to my house until he was dry," Scooter answered.

"It was better to be late than be caught doing something I was told not to do. Either way, I was grounded for a week." I smiled, finishing Scooter's story.

The faint sound of rushing water began to grow as we approached the first set of rapids.

"Oh crap, they're huge," Todd yelled. "Now what?"

"Stay close and do as I do," Parker answered calmly.

Parker and Buck took the lead position and used their hands to paddle to what looked like the best course to navigate the rapids. As they moved to the center, they yelled back to us that the coast was clear. Just a quick way to let us know there didn't appear to be any large boulders protruding out of the water, only white caps about a foot or two in height. I followed next with Todd on my heels. As we paddled into position, our speed increased. We entered the rapids and bobbed up and down several times. I heard Todd yelling like a child at an amusement park. It didn't last long, less than a minute, and once again, we were on a calm, lazy stretch of the creek.

Wildman brought up the rear, yelling his head off the entire way down the rapids. He kept his hands over his head. I guess that was his way of letting us know he was a daredevil.

"Yeah! That's way too cool," shouted Todd as he threw his fist into the air. "Oh yeah! Bring on the next one, baby! Woo!"

"Don't you worry; there are plenty more to come," I told him.

"That was a baby compared to the ones coming up," Parker snickered.

Todd sat quietly for a minute; he must have been wondering what lay ahead. The rest of us stretched out and began to relax. We had another thirty minutes or so before the next set would be nipping at our heels. We spotted a few deer grazing on the banks of the creek, which halted our light conversations. Four deer, all of them does, lifting their graceful necks to gaze at us. Then stepping out from behind the brush, a nice eight-point buck appeared. Scooter and I explained to Todd the difference. The does were the females, and the buck was the male. We explained that it was eight points, one each for every point on its antlers. Todd seemed impressed; he savored the view. I think he was starting to like living in the country.

Time passed, and the water started to move at a faster rate. We were heading into a long bend. On the right, we were surrounded by towering forty-foot cliffs. On the left, was a four to five-foot embankment. Parker and Buck signaled to us to be quiet. We slowly made our way to the far side of the cliffs, hugging them the best we could. It was old man Smithers' place.

As long as we stayed quiet and let the current take us past, the old man wouldn't even know we were there.

Then I noticed something different. Old man Smithers had got himself a dog. We looked back and forth at each other. I guess we were trying to figure out what to do. Parker reacted first by lying flat on his raft with the hopes the dog might not see him; some of us followed his lead. The water speed increased, small ripples for waves. We were moving at a good rate of speed. At this pace, we would pass the quarter mile stretch that Smithers owned in no time.

The small dog ran to the edge of the grass and began barking as we floated past. Buck raised a finger to his lips and tried to shush the dog. He pleaded for it to be quiet, but that didn't work. The sound of the screen door slamming against the house was the next sound I heard. Along with the pounding of footsteps of old man Smithers running to see why his new pet was barking.

Then he noticed us, and turning quickly, he made a mad dash for the house, yelling the entire way, "I warned you boys not to trespass on my property!" Buck, Parker, and the rest of us, still lying flat, began to paddle frantically. Panic raced through my veins. We were almost free and clear when the sound of the screen door slammed again.

Old man Smithers fast approached, yelling, "I warned you, boys." He pulled up his shotgun to fire a warning shot in the air. I'm pretty sure it was only buck shot. The loud sound rang out and echoed off the cliff walls. Birds scattered from the trees, and we all started screaming and yelling for him to stop. We paddled faster. No one would think twice about hearing gunfire coming from the woods. I'm sure they would think it was a hunter. I thought about telling my dad or the authorities, but I wasn't sure anyone would believe us.

So we did the only thing we could. I paddled faster while others rolled into the water and took cover behind their rafts as they continued kicking in the water. The old man had completely lost his marbles this time. One by one, we faded out of sight and drifted farther away from his property. Another round of gunfire rang out, echoing off the canyon walls.

"He won't chase us into the woods, will he?" asked Todd.

"I don't think so," Parker said when we heard a final warning shot ring out.

The faint sounds of Old Man Smithers' yelling and his barking dog grew further away. The water began to slow and settle into another long calm stretch.

Chapter Ten

Slowly coming into view was one of the bridges we had walked across on our journey to the launch site. The area around the bridge was a nice place to swim. We stored the rafts under the bridge on the embankment.

"Let's stop and swim," announced Parker.

Todd looked around a bit, up at the bridge and back toward old man Smithers' house. I could tell something was bothering him. "So we could have launched from here instead of being shot at by that crazy old fart?" He was upset and had every right to be.

"Yes, but that would have cut an hour off our trip, plus look at all the fun we already had." Parker grinned. He was pretty convincing, and Todd let it drop quickly. He launched into how great this bridge was to Todd. This place brought back good memories for Parker and Buck. They both had been swimming here the past two summers. Wildman and I had only been here once, and this was Scooter's and Todd's first time.

Once the rafts were secure, Parker took off, quickly making his way topside. Buck joined him, followed by the rest of us. Parker looked left then right. No cars or trucks were coming. He placed one foot up on the guardrail and then stepped up with the other. Standing on the top railing, he paused and stretched his arms to his sides and looked down at the clear blue water under the bridge; it was crisp, clean, and about twelve feet deep, perfect for jumping.

"Woo hoo!" Parker yelled as he leaped from the bridge. The twenty-foot drop made quite the splash when he entered the water.

Buck was next to climb, and without hesitation he jumped and then splashed into the water. He surfaced, waved to the rest of us to let them know he was safe, and made his way up the bank for another jump.

Once he cleared the landing area, Wildman Jimmy made his way to the top rail, saying he always felt like he was one of those cliff divers from Acapulco that he and his father watched on TV. He looked around for a second and then waved to the crowd. He raised both of his hands straight out to the side and eased them over his head. I watched him push off, tucking as he flipped from the top railing. He had somersaulted in midair before his near perfect landing in the water, with only a minimal amount of a splash.

"Give the boy a ten," shouted Parker. I guess he had forgotten all about the little skirmish the two had earlier in the day.

I gazed into the deep pool of water, and that's when I spotted Jimmy. He didn't appear to be moving. *What's he doing? What's taking so long? Could something be wrong?* I then noticed he had started waving his hands and arms around.

"Something's wrong. I think he's stuck," I yelled to the others. They all gazed up at me. I don't think they heard me, and if they did, they obviously didn't know what I was yelling. No one moved to help Jimmy, who remained below the surface. I gazed down again. I could only make out bits and pieces, and it looked like Jimmy was trying to free himself from whatever was holding him. I was about to jump when Jimmy came shooting out of the water, gasping for air.

"Something pulled me down, and I couldn't shake it loose," Wildman yelled as he swam to the water's edge.

"I didn't see anything," Buck responded.

"I don't know; it felt like someone was keeping me there," Jimmy gasped as he tried shaking it off and then began to crawl his way back up the embankment.

Once Wildman was out of the water, I shouted, "All clear." I jumped without being told or pushed like my brother had done to me the year before. I wasn't afraid even after Jimmy's little episode in the water; he'd been known to pull stunts like that to gain attention.

Todd looked over the railing and turned to Parker, who had made his way back to the top of the bridge. "Time to jump, big guy," Parker said as he softly punched Todd in the arm.

"It's safe, right? What about Jimmy?" Todd asked.

"Jimmy's fine. If it wasn't safe, we wouldn't do it. Besides, he was just playing like he always does." Todd nodded and took a step up on the railing, and without thinking, he jumped, yelling the whole way down and stopping only when he entered the water.

"You're next, Scooter," Parker shouted.

"I'm good," he answered.

"What?" a bewildered Parker answered.

"Come on. We all did it," Buck begged.

"Yeah, come on!" I yelled up at him.

Scooter looked over the railing and watched as Todd swam to the bank. Todd stopped and sat down, looked up, and yelled, "It's not that bad. Come on, Scooter."

"Come on, man. You can do it. Don't be afraid," Jimmy coached him.

Scooter placed a foot on the railing and then slowly placed another foot up. Laying his hands on the railing, he lowered himself over. "I think I'll move down a little to the steel beams," he said confidently.

Parker and Buck whispered something to each other as they stepped closer to the edge and looked down as Scooter made his way down five feet to the lower level.

"You got this; it's easy," Todd called from below.

Then I chimed in, "Yeah, don't be a putz."

"You've got this, dude," Jimmy shouted as we watched from the shoreline.

Scooter was now on the lower beam, positioned fifteen feet above the water with a light breeze in the air, but I couldn't figure out what was taking so long. Parker and Buck each took a step up on the upper railing. They looked around making sure no cars were coming. Then they looked back down to see if Scooter had jumped.

"Come on, Scooter; just jump," said Buck.

Scooter looked up at the two. "I don't think I can do this. I'm scared."

"You can't come back up. We won't let you," Buck replied in a stern voice.

"Please, I can't do this," he pleaded.

"Yes, you can. It's time to be a man. Now, let go of the bridge and jump," said Buck.

"I can't, I... I just can't," Scooter begged. "Please let me back up?"

Parker took another step up to the top railing. Looking down at Scooter, he unzipped his shorts and yelled, "Dude, you'd better jump. I'm going to pee."

We all hollered. I was the first. "That's gross, man."

Todd sat mesmerized. It looked like he couldn't believe what he was seeing as Parker positioned himself right over Scooter who was now on the verge of crying. We all yelled. Some yelled jump; others yelled for Parker to stop. Buck was the only one to cheer him on. Only making matters worse.

"Don't make me jump," Scooter pleaded again.

"I'm gonna start. I feel it," bellowed Parker.

Just as Parker was about to go, Scooter found his nerve and let go of the steel beam, screaming all the way down. He sounded like a little girl as he made his way into the water.

There was a loud plop when Scooter landed, followed by a giant splash.

We all cheered for Scooter with shouts of "You're the man! Dyno-mite!" and "Way to go!" Scooter swam to the water's edge and then as he pulled himself up on the embankment, he looked up at Parker and shouted, "You're a real ass, you know that? I should kick your ..."

Parker cut him off midsentence as he looked down. In response, he shouted back, "You know I wasn't going to do it, man. You know that, right? I was only kidding."

"Sure," Todd said. "It looked like you were going to do it from down here."

"I just wanted him to be part of the group," Parker added as he waved his hands to let us know he didn't care what we thought.

"Maybe it's time to move on," said Buck as he stepped up on the top railing and jumped. He grabbed a knee, leaned back just a little to form what we called a "jackknife," a different type of cannonball that was meant to make a big splash. As he entered the creek, a large plume of water shot straight up into the air; it was so high it almost touched the bottom of the bridge.

"Watch this one," Parker yelled as he did the same, trying to one up Buck. It was almost a tie, but I think Parker's splash may have touched the bridge.

Jimmy had made his way back up top and was going to try it again, despite what happened on his last attempt. We were all under the bridge, sitting on the bank waiting for his last jump to see if he could break the record for the largest splash. Parker's record was safe that afternoon as Jimmy came up a little short.

Scooter was still upset with Parker. Most of it was dismissed as Parker just having a little fun. Todd was the only one that wasn't that happy because he wasn't sure what Parker would have done.

The minutes passed, and we were ready to move on. Pushing the rafts back into the water, we once again made our way downstream, talking and laughing as we bragged about our jumps when I noticed two large crows watching us from the far side of the creek. They sat in silence, observing us as we floated away. Jimmy pulled up along the side of me. He glanced at the crows and then turned to me. He told me that he had caught a glimpse of a bright light in the water as he entered. He said he could make out the image. It was Annabelle standing on the rocks of the creek bed. "She asked me if I had the box."

"I froze. I wasn't sure what to do, I just shook my head no."

'It's mine, and I want it back,' she hissed at me," Jimmy explained.

"I didn't take anything; it was given to me," he responded, but he ended up taking a large gulp of water. Realizing he was under water, he panicked. He waved his arms trying to get away. Something seemed to be holding him there. He couldn't explain it.

Finally, he planted his foot firmly on the bottom, pushed off, and swam upward.

"Where are you going?" He heard her scream as she tried to grab his ankle. The last thing he heard was, "Consider this your final warning!"

"Dude, she knows I have the puzzle box."

I didn't know what to say except, "Relax, we'll figure this out."

Jimmy took a couple of deep breaths as we tried to catch up with the others.

Chapter Eleven

Wildman finally seemed a little calmer. As we approached the next bend, another set of rapids came into view. They appeared to take a steep drop downward and looked to be much larger and faster than the first ones. We noticed a few large boulders rising above the water line and immediately knew right away shooting the rapids would be trickier. Buck and Parker took the lead again, searching for the best line to travel. The creek cut through the large jagged boulders that lined both sides of the steep embankments. The sun was darting in and out, and the clouds began to build, casting shadows over the water. Buck and Parker hollered as they bobbed up and down the rapids. They looked like two guys riding a seesaw at the local playground. They made their way through the rapids and then disappeared into a pool at the bottom.

I was next to follow, and Todd stayed right on my heels. There was nothing better than the feeling when you first entered the rapids. The water seemed to blend to form a funnel-type effect. The speed of the raft increased as the force of the water pulled us downstream. The raft dipped down and then quickly rose upward. The breaks were a good three feet, and several more lay ahead. Paddling to the left, I just missed a large boulder. Todd did the same, skimming the edge of one. My adrenaline was pumping. A few more up and down motions, and this wild ride was over.

Looking back upstream, I could see Scooter had begun to make his descent with Wildman not far behind. The view looked different from the lower side, not as bouncy, more like a child's roller coaster versus the large adult rides, but when you were in the middle of the rapids, you could feel the real force of the water. One mistake, and your life could be over. One second Scooter was there, and the next he was gone as Wildman appeared, holding his arms in the air. They looked like two puppets going up and down, one up as the other vanished.

In one split second, everything changed. Wildman struck one of the rocks and slipped out of sight. What seemed like minutes was only seconds before Jimmy bobbed up, and we could tell he had somehow managed to stay on his raft. A large chunk of the Styrofoam had broken off and swirled in the moving water next to him. The raft was still in decent shape as he neared the bottom of the rushing waters. Scooter made it down fine and in one piece.

"Woo, what a ride," yelled Wildman as he pumped his fist in the air. "Man, was I booking it or what?"

"I thought you were gonna bite the big one for a second," I admitted.

"Not a chance," smirked Jimmy.

"You're just one lucky cat, that's all," Parker squawked.

"No, he's a lucky shit," Buck stage-whispered to Parker; he was far enough away that some of the others probably didn't hear.

Wildman and I looked over his raft to make sure he could continue. Todd paddled over to offer assistance. I think he just wanted to see the damage. Everything looked to be in perfect working order except for the ten-inch chunk that was missing from the front left side.

"This may sound crazy, and trust me, I'm not—," Jimmy said to me before he was cut off.

"What are you babbling about now," Parker yelled.

"Nothing, I was just telling Johnny what a ride it was."

Jimmy turned back to me and whispered, "Someone pushed me into the boulder. It even sounds strange when I say it out loud. I did everything I could." He took a shuddering breath, and I noticed the fear in his eyes.

I could tell Jimmy was agitated and upset. Maybe it was fatigue, or maybe it was something else altogether. I struggled to believe his story, but on the other hand, there seemed to be too many coincidences to ignore.

"I wish I would have never taken that puzzle box from Tom Evans," he confessed.

"I don't have any answers for you. Maybe it's the story Parker told last night that has you a little spooked," I insisted.

"I don't think so. I guess, ah… maybe… I mean, ah man," Wildman said as he shook his head in frustration. "Let's move on, and please don't tell the others."

"Deal," I said, wondering if Jimmy was making this up just to play some trick on me later. It wouldn't be the first time he'd done that. I thought back to last Halloween when Jimmy knocked on the door at our house, and when I opened it, a pumpkin exploded on the front porch.

We approached the quarry. On the left, the tall rocky bluffs shot straight up in the air as if they were reaching for the stars. We all lay on our backs and gazed upward at the large rock formations

Occasionally, a downed tree would stretch out into the water. Some of them contained a turtle or two. Others seemed to have large spider webs. We were all star struck when we spotted a large, yellow zipper spider occupying its web between two large branches on one of the trees. We were never sure if zipper spider was the correct name, but that's what it looked like, a giant zipper right down the middle of the web.

"Hey, did you see that?" Jimmy broke the silence as he pointed toward the left side of the bank.

I noticed Jimmy was trembling. "What's up, dude? What'd you see?" I asked.

Wildman hesitated as he turned to me. "It's… her. She's over there." Pointing toward the trees.

"Who?" I asked, craning my neck to see what Jimmy saw.

"You know, man, her, Annabelle." He nodded his head.

"No, I'm sorry. I don't see anything," I replied.

"Hey, are you two going to catch up?" Parker yelled from about fifty yards downstream.

"We're coming!" I hollered back.

Jimmy turned to me once again. "Dude, you have to believe me when I say I saw Annabelle. She was right over there." Jimmy's voice shook; he was obviously frightened.

"Are you sure?" I asked, trying my best to believe him.

"I kid you not, dude. She warned me last night, then today at the bridge and the rapids. She's after me," said a quite shaken Jimmy.

"Why would she be after you?" I questioned.

"That damn puzzle box. It belonged to her," he replied.

I assured Wildman he must be seeing things and that the bridge incident was just a coincidence and nothing more. Just like at the rapids, how could she push him into the boulder? In the back of my mind, I wasn't convinced, and I didn't think I had swayed Jimmy either. Worse yet, I began to wonder about this box and what made it so special. I couldn't wait to get my hands on it. But now it was time to catch up with the others.

Chapter Twelve

The water lay perfectly still. You could have skipped a stone across the surface. I think Parker held the record for skipping stones, with twelve. My best was eight, from what I can remember. When Parker told the story, he made it sound like his best record was a hundred or so, but we all knew better.

The clouds continued to dart in and out. There was a light breeze in the air, and when the clouds rolled over, the temperature felt like it had dropped twenty degrees. The day was picture perfect, a scene right out of the movies.

The smell of freshly cut lumber soon filled the air. We could see the sawmill coming into view. Jimmy's house sat right next to the edge of the tall stacks of logs that made up the landscape. Jimmy wanted to stop for a few minutes to take care of something important. None of us minded; the stop would give us a chance to dry off and raid his refrigerator. We pulled ourselves to the edge of the creek, quickly made our way up the grassy riverbank, and stashed the makeshift rafts under some large bushes so they would not be seen by the workers at the lumberyard or be blown away by an unexpected wind. The workers didn't like Jimmy because of the tricks he'd played on them, and we knew if they spotted the foam rafts, they would have broken them to pieces and thrown them into the creek.

We snuck around the far left side and hid behind large stacks of lumber. I had always loved the scent of fresh cut pine. We followed Wildman as we made our way to the basement door. Pushing the door open, one by one, we entered the home.

His parents both worked, but this was a Saturday, and the chances were good they were both in the house. The five of us remained silent and hung out in the basement while Jimmy went upstairs. It felt like he was taking forever.

About fifteen minutes later, the basement door swung open, and we heard the sound of footsteps pounding down the stairs. It was Wildman with the remains of a sandwich hanging out of his mouth. He was also carrying a six-pack of Pepsi and a large bag of Middleswarth potato chips, a Pennsylvania favorite. He handed each of us a bottle, holding onto one for himself. Five hands sprung for the bag of chips all at once, almost knocking them out of his hands and all over the floor. We acted like we hadn't eaten in weeks. He gestured to us by holding his hands out to each side, a way to signal for all of us to back off. Then he pointed upstairs. We nodded our heads to let him know that we understood this was not a time to be making noise or acting like a bunch of fools because his parents were home. Once we calmed down, we all enjoyed the taste of those special barbecue-flavored chips.

The crunching and slurping sounds lasted only a few minutes before everything grew silent. In no time at all, everything was polished off. We were now ready to return to the creek.

Jimmy seemed a little nervous as we started back toward the lumberyard. I could tell something was bothering him.

"You all right, man?" I asked.

Nodding, Jimmy replied, "I'm good now. I had to take care of something before it was too late."

"Did you get the puzzle box?"

"Now's not the time," he said under his breath as he made his way to the door.

The six of us quietly snuck past the large stacks of logs. Then a commotion broke out, and we heard screaming and yelling. The sounds were coming from the lumber yard. My worst fear had come true; they had spotted us and were running in our direction. I'm sure they thought we were up to no good. We heard them approaching quickly. "Run!" Parker yelled.

We took off as fast as we could, dodging left and right as we wound our way toward the creek. Three large men gave chase, but the six of us were small and agile when it came to running through the brush. Parker, Buck, and Todd broke off and made a mad dash for the creek. Jimmy, Scooter, and I took cover under a large bush, stopping briefly to catch our breath. We could see the older boys had made it to the creek. We watched them grab all the rafts and barrel into the water. The three men stood on the bank yelling at them. The three of us took off in the other direction and quietly trekked upstream, taking cover behind several large bushes. Just a few more yards and we would be safe. We sprinted the last little stretch to the edge and bounced into the water.

"That was close," Jimmy howled.

We knew they chased us because of Jimmy. The six of us were safe now and back in the water. Three men stood along the bank yelling when they spotted us meeting up with the others.

The late afternoon sun was bright and shone down on the creek. The bright glare was almost blinding the way it reflected off the water. Parker explained to Todd that we weren't that far from the camp now. We had this long stretch of the creek to go and then past the island rapids, where we would have to choose which side to go down. At the same time, Buck was doing damage control with Scooter. I faintly heard him try to reassure Scooter that Parker was only playing back at the bridge. Jimmy and I brought up the rear of the flotilla.

Thirty minutes passed before the island formed in the middle of the creek. It was a good-sized island, about forty feet wide in some places and a little longer than the length of a football field. Dense foliage covered the island, which was made up mainly of small ten-foot trees and shrubs. We had stopped there from time to time, acting out Columbus staking his claim when he discovered a new strange land. The creek split in half here, and each side made its way around the small land mass. One of the sections of the creek was about twenty feet wide and flowed at a nice steady speed, with nothing more than one to two-foot whitecaps.

The other side was rough and contained a steep drop; it also had some of the largest rapids that the creek had to offer. Considering the circumstances, we always accepted the challenge and went down the rough side.

Like always, Parker and Buck were the first two to enter the "vortex," as they liked to call it. The point of no return. Of course, we all exaggerated a little. Parker rode the waves up and down and made his way past the island.

Buck was next to enter. I heard him mention he was worried about his raft, that he wasn't sure it would hold up on the four to five-foot waves. The ride was smooth that day and uneventful, as he glided to the bottom of the rapids.

Scooter may have been afraid to jump off the bridge, but shooting the rapids was something that he had become accustomed to as he cleared the long stretch of whitecaps.

I asked Todd to go next. This way, Wildman or I would be right behind to rescue him just in case he was to run into any issues. But like the others, Todd made it through, coming out at the end in one piece.

As expected, I had no issues riding the massive waves before entering the calm, clear pool on the lower side. I wondered if I should have gone last this time because of all the bad luck Jimmy had been having. We saw Wildman enter the rapids with his hands held straight up in the air. Then they were gone, then up again as he came to the top of the next wave, and then once again, he was gone. This ride was uneventful, just smooth sailing for all of us as we started down the home stretch. The large, slow moving area would lead to one more small set of rapids before we would arrive back at camp.

If the bear hasn't returned to finish off the rest of the fish, I'm going to cook'em all up before trying to catch anymore. Along with cooking the rest of the beans! I was just that hungry, and I figured the rest of the guys were, too.

Our group drifted a little farther, inching closer toward camp when a loud rustling sound came from the north side of the embankment. Wildman, still a little jittery, was the first one to hear it, followed by me. Parker and Buck weren't sure they heard anything. Todd pointed in the direction of a large bush that seemed to be moving. Scooter completely ignored whatever it was; he just wanted to get back to camp so he could eat.

Parker reached to the bottom of the shallow water and pulled out a baseball sized rock. In one swift motion, he tossed it in the direction of the bush. The throw came up a little short, splashing at the water's edge before sinking into the mud and making a funny sucking sound. Reaching down again, he pulled up another one. Then Buck, Todd, and Wildman all joined in, sailing rocks in the direction of the large shrubs.

"Wait, hold up," I yelled. "Parker, what if it's your sisters?" My thoughts quickly turned to Sara and Lexi. The others ignored me, and the rocks continued to fly.

The movement behind the bush came to a stop. Parker held up his hands and signaled to stop throwing. Maybe it was nothing or just some small animal, like a muskrat or beaver. Parker motioned with his hands for all of us to move in, so we paddled toward the bank. Buck, Todd, and Wildman were right on his heels. They were all curious as to what they might find lurking behind the shrubs.

The four of them surrounded the bush on all sides. I stayed back a little and watched. Parker nodded and moved his head to signal the others to move in on the target. They quickly rushed the bush all at the same time. The leaves rustled as several quail flew out and startled them. They all jumped back, followed by some screaming and yelling that quickly turned to laughter as they sat at the water's edge. Scooter and I paddled over to see if they needed any help.

Chapter Thirteen

We made our final stop. Now it was time to head toward camp. Parker and Buck talked about who had fish gutting detail, who would collect firewood, and who would do the cooking. It was funny how none of the chores that were required around camp had anything to do with them. With age came privileges, I supposed.

Once we cleared the last small set of rapids, Parker and Buck paddled to the bank, let go of their Styrofoam rafts, and watched them float down the creek. The environmentalist today would have nightmares watching these large pieces of non-biodegradable foam just float away, but back then, we were young and had never really given the environment much thought; I guess it was the times.

Todd and Scooter were next to pull into shore, and they released their rafts back to the wild. I was next to dismount my raft and set it free. Jimmy was still floating down the middle of the creek, making no attempt to come to shore.

Cupping my hands around my mouth, I yelled, "Hey!"

Wildman offered no response. He seemed to be in a daze or trance. Todd and Scooter noticed that Jimmy was still in the water when they came back to the embankment and joined me in yelling at him.

"Let him sink," Parker yelled.

"Yeah, what a jerk!" said Buck.

"Something's wrong," I yelled. I could feel it in my bones. Jimmy wasn't responding, and that wasn't like him to ignore everyone. Scooter, Todd, and I began to walk along the water's edge keeping pace with Jimmy as we continued to yell in hopes of getting his attention. Nothing seemed to shake him out of the spell. Jimmy floated on downstream as if he didn't have a care in the world. We continued to walk alongside the creek, going farther and farther away from camp.

The current began to increase. Jimmy sat still, right in the middle of his raft. We picked up our pace as we tried to keep up with Jimmy. We were in uncharted territory; none of us had ever floated down this far, and Jimmy was less than a mile from what remained of the dam.

Parker and Buck finally joined the chase. After all, they were the oldest, and they knew if something happened to Jimmy, they would be held responsible. The two ran as fast as they could, trying to catch up to the rest of us.

"What are we going to do?" I yelled, panic lacing my voice.

"Look for some long branches. Maybe we can reach him with one," replied Scooter.

"No, it looks like the creek's getting wider as we get closer to the dam," said Todd.

"Follow me," I yelled and sprinted off to get ahead the raft while we still had time. Todd bolted quickly, staying stride for stride on my heels. Scooter fell slightly behind; he didn't have the energy to keep up with the rest of us. Parker and Buck soon caught up to Scooter and began yelling at Jimmy.

"What's wrong with this cat?" Parker yelled in frustration.

"Is he on something? Did anyone see him take anything?" accused Buck.

"I don't get it!" Parker yelled.

Todd and I arrived at the dam and then hustled to the far side where the water flowed over the broken spillway. We darted out onto the larger rocks that reached into the water. The creek was only twenty feet across at this point, and the current was at its strongest. The water pushed together like the sand draining from an hour glass, creating a force stronger than any of us had ever experienced.

"If we only had some rope or something that would stretch to the other side," I said aloud, thinking as quickly as I could. I knew time was running out, and we needed a plan, or something bad was going to happen.

"Even if we had some rope, how would one of us get to the other side to hold it?" Todd replied frantically.

"Good point, I don't know. Think, man, think!" I yelled at myself as I clutched my hands over my head and bent over at the waist. My friend was in trouble, and I didn't know how to save him. *Keep calm, and stay focused.* "Wait, we have some rope in the tower," I whispered to myself. I took off in a full sprint toward the concrete stairs that lead to the control room.

"Where ya going, man?" Todd yelled as he spun around and watched me bolt up the stairs.

I was exhausted. Sweat beaded on my forehead and dripped down the side of my cheeks, but I pushed myself harder to get to the top. *One step at a time, one foot in front of the other, just keep moving, you can do this.* I burst into the large control room high above what remained of the dam. "Where is it? Where did we put that damn rope?" I yelled, trying to think.

I knew that time was of the essence. "Oh wait," I shouted as I yanked open the doors on the bottom cabinets, at least, the ones that had doors. I flung the doors open to get a glance inside, and some of the rotten wood broke and flew across the room. I continued ripping open the doors as fast as I could. *How many damn doors are in this place!* My mind raced as I went from one door to the next, opening and slamming them shut. *Wait...* then it hit me. We had hidden the rope so no one would find it, along with the soda bottles.

I quickly glanced out the large open-framed window. Then I spared a glance toward the creek. I could see Jimmy coming into view, fast approaching the spillway, less than a quarter mile away. Panic set in as I darted to the other side of the room. Bending over, I began pulling up some loose boards and revealed our hideaway spot. Several soda bottles were there, which I cast aside, not caring if they broke. I heard the bottles clang on the hard concrete floor. A sigh of relief came over me as I wrapped my hands around a large piece or rope. I pulled it from the bottom of the box and sprinted toward the door.

I burst outside and yelled down to Todd, "I found it! I found it!" Excitement oozing out of me, I dashed down the stairs, tripping several times over my feet. I didn't care; nothing mattered. I had one thing on my mind, which was to save my friend. Todd met me at the bottom and eyed the large bundle of rope in my hands.

"Tie this around me," he shouted as he grabbed the rope.

"I don't think I can hold you," I shouted back, frustrated.

We both turned to look upstream. We could see Jimmy fast approaching as well as Buck, Parker, and Scooter jogging alongside the embankment. Todd and I jumped up and down, yelling and screaming at the others. We frantically waved our hands trying to motion them to run faster and get to the dam. I held the rope high in the air for the others to see, trying to encourage them to run faster and to show them that we had a plan to rescue Jimmy.

They must have noticed what I had in my hands because Buck and Parker broke into a full sprint toward the dam. Scooter was just plum out of breath and fell farther and farther behind. He couldn't even keep up with Jimmy at this point. He stopped a few times, placed his hands on his knees, and gulped for air while the speed of the water steadily increased, pushing Jimmy closer to the spillway. None of us had ever gone over before, not on a raft, not even a canoe. I flashed back thinking about what my parents had once told me: "Never swim near the dam; the currents are too strong. It will pull you under, and you will most certainly drown!" Fear raced in my blood.

I spotted Scooter change directions, and he was running faster than I thought he could, but he wasn't coming toward the dam. No, he must have decided to get Mr. Parker. Bobby Parker's father would know what to do, as long as he wasn't drunk. After all, it was Saturday.

Jimmy rapidly approached the spillway, which was now less than a hundred yards away. The creek was narrowing in on the sides from thirty feet wide to twenty-five, and soon it would only be twenty. The water was getting deeper, and the currents were much too strong to paddle to the side at this point. Jimmy slowly glanced toward Todd and me, looking straight at us, expressionless as if he didn't have a care in the world.

A dark cloud passed overhead, casting an ominous shadow over the creek. Two large crows flew in and settled in the tree on the far side, just ahead of the steep six-foot drop. They squawked several times loudly as they loomed over the water.

I noticed the crows, and thoughts of Jimmy's stories raced through my mind. *Did the crows have something to do with what was happening to Jimmy? Were they sitting there cheering for him? Even worse, could they be making him do this? Or could it be the work of Annabelle?* A helpless feeling sank over me as I watched Jimmy approach the falls.

Todd said he was good with a rope because he had spent an entire summer working on a dude ranch in Texas. He learned to lasso a wooden post and a young calf that was secured to the railing but never something moving at this speed. However, after a quick discussion, we all felt he was our best shot at saving Jimmy. Of course, the best-case scenario would be for Jimmy and his raft to flow over the spillway safely and continue downstream until the water calmed down.

Parker, Buck, and I gathered as close as we could to the water's edge at the base of the dam and braced our feet against some large pieces of concrete. The roar of the water pouring over the old spillway was deafening, making it hard for us to hear each other. The three of us held the rope as tightly as we could while Todd stepped out onto a large piece of damaged concrete that stuck out over the water.

We braced ourselves as Jimmy rapidly approached; he was now only fifty feet away and closing in fast. The hairs on the back of my neck stood on end as I watched helplessly. Trying to get a feel for the rope, Todd began swinging the rope in a circle over his head and made a practice toss out over the creek. He muttered that the rope was much thicker than the rope he used on the ranch. He glared at the spot where the rope landed. He quickly pulled it back as fast as he could and started circling the rope over his head. The raft was almost to the top of the spillway. I could see Jimmy's eyes were pitch black, a stark contrast against his skin, and showed no fear as he approached.

I could tell by the expression on his face that he was in a trance or possessed or maybe even hypnotized by something or someone. Everything grew silent, the sounds of the birds vanished, and the wind settled. Only the roar of the water flowing over the spillway could be heard.

Time slowed down, seconds passed, but they felt like hours. Todd continued to swing the rope above his head. The rest of us leaned back and braced ourselves the best we could against the large pieces of debris. Deep down, I think we all knew it wasn't going to be easy pulling Wildman back to shore against the force of the water.

The first thing was for Todd to lasso him, but what if he missed? Thoughts raced through my mind. *Could Jimmy snap out of whatever spell he was under long enough to grab the rope? Did he even want to be saved?*

The time was now; Jimmy had reached the top of the spillway. Todd, like an eagle circling its prey, watched and stayed focused on his target. His hand flew forward, and I watched the rope fly over the water. The loop shot over its target, but part of the rope lay across the front half of the raft. We screamed at Jimmy to grab the rope, but he never moved. He seemed lifeless, amazed by the water before him. Todd pulled the rope back trying to snag an arm or a leg before the raft took the plunge over the spillway.

The raft raced down the steep incline. A loud cracking sound filled the air as the raft plunged to the bottom. The Styrofoam broke into several pieces, plummeting Jimmy into the swirling waters. At first, we could see him. Once, twice, three times he bobbed up and down, like a bobber on a fishing line that had hooked a fish.

Our screams urging Jimmy to grab the rope could be heard over the roar of the water. It lay on the surface within Jimmy's grasp, but he never moved. The strong underwater currents forced him below the surface. The last thing I remember was his hand before it went below the water. Now trapped in the undertow, the water pulled him to the floor of the creek. The force of the water held him there, making it impossible to reach the surface. We don't know if Jimmy ever tried. I think he closed his eyes for the final time.

Parker, Buck, and I stood in silence. Six eyes glued to the water, frantically looking for any signs of life. We waited for him to resurface. Time was slipping by. Something had to be done, but what? Parker and Buck stood frozen like statues, not sure what to do. Todd came back off the rocks and looked on as he and the rest us watched several pieces of his raft drift downstream. We searched back and forth trying to spot him.

Todd instantly sprang into action, quickly wrapping the rope around his waist before he tied it in a flimsy knot. He turned to us, his eyes wide, reflecting the fear we all felt. "Don't let go. Please, don't let go," he pleaded. That was the last thing he said as he dove into the water. Todd bobbed up and down. Then he dove down searching for Jimmy in the dark waters. The last thing we saw was Todd's feet raising in the air before they were submerged.

Parker, Buck, and I held on for dear life and were holding onto our hopes that Todd would resurface with Jimmy in his arms. Fifteen long seconds had passed before Todd came back up for air. He took a big gulp and then submerged himself again. He was drifting farther downstream himself. The currents pushed him away from the dam and still no sign of the Wildman. The only thing that remained was a few pieces of foam that were floating away fast.

Parker's father was running quickly across the path. I could hear him yell. "Get him out of the water! Pull him out now!" he kept shouting as he approached.

I watched Scooter try to keep up with the older man before his steps slowed to a defeated stop. The look on his face told me he realized that Jimmy hadn't resurfaced yet. I heard Mr. Parker yell back at Scooter to go back and call the police. When Mr. Parker turned back to look at us, his face was pale, confirming what we all feared, that Jimmy was gone.

Parker's father came over, grabbed the rope, and hollered for all of us to pull. "We've lost one today, but we're not losing two!" he barked as he urged us to pull harder. We pulled and pulled, resembling a tug of war contest, only this time the stakes were much higher. At first, Todd tried to fight us as he waved his hand to stop pulling and tried to dive again. He was tired and the current too strong, so little by little, we pulled Todd to the lower edge of the dam walkway.

Stretching his hand out, Parker's father grabbed Todd's arm and pulled him to safety on the large concrete slab.

Todd tried to fight and kick, wanting to go back in the water and try one more time to rescue Jimmy, but Mr. Parker held firm and wouldn't let go as he stood in silence, his jaw gaping in disbelief. Buck stood looking downstream, his eyes silently pleading that Jimmy would resurface. I dropped down, landing on my butt, and rocked back and forth with my head on my knees, my hands fisting in my hair. The only sounds I could hear were my screams and sobs as I mourned my best friend.

Lexi and Sara approached the creek. Stopping once, Lexi pointed, and her eyes darted back and forth surveying the scene. She looked again, screamed, "Where's Jimmy," and then burst into tears.

Sara dropped to her knees. I could tell she was in shock as tears flowed down her face. Quickly, she moved her hands to cover her mouth and then let out a loud scream.

Mr. Parker rustled the older boys together as he yelled, "What were you thinking? This is nuts, insane!"

"Dad," Parker cried, "we tried. We all pulled out of the creek back at camp, but Jimmy didn't. He didn't want to stop. He kept going. We tried, we tried, we…" He broke down mid sentence and started to cry. Mr. Parker pulled him close, hugging him like never before.

"It's all right; it's all right," he repeated over and over, not wanting to let go of his son as he rubbed his back.

Our father was the next to arrive and frantically looked to find Buck and me. Spotting us, he quickly ran, grabbed Buck first, and pulled him into his arms. Then he helped me to my feet and pulled me tightly into his body. I could sense some relief rushing over him, followed by guilt. All he wanted was to comfort us boys and help take away our pain.

Everything after that seemed like a blur, like a dream that you can't remember, no matter how hard you try. The police arrived along with the fire department. Several scuba divers went into the water and began their search for the missing boy.

* * *

I paused, took in a deep breath, and wiped a few tears from my eyes. Daniel sat in silence, and a tear ran down his cheek. Seeing the pain in my eyes, he turned and laid a hand on my knee. "Are you all right?"

"I'll be fine," I said wiping another tear from my cheek. "The story just brought back some bad memories; I lost my best friend that day." I sighed. "I'll be fine," I said and wiped another tear with the back of my hand.

"Is this story true?" whispered Zack.

"That part is," I responded and took another deep breath. The boys could tell I was hurting. They weren't sure how to help.

I thought I was over the pain of Jimmy's loss. I guess I was wrong. I paused for a moment, cleared my throat, and continued my story.

Chapter Fourteen

Days passed. The pain of losing someone so close was overwhelming. To think you will never see that person again. Never hear him laugh or see him smile, never play hide and seek, or climb the logs at the lumberyard. There would be no more camping or fishing trips, no more Halloweens, birthdays, or Christmas parties together. All gone in one split second. One moment the person was there; the next he was not. Life is short, they say. That summer we learned how short it could be.

The day of the funeral arrived. There was standing room only at the funeral home. Flower arrangements lined the walls; up front, a small, black casket remained closed. Sitting on top was a large picture of Jimmy. To the sides of the caskets were several more pictures of him.

Local kids from school, along with their parents, filled the room. Mr. Evans was there, dressed in a nice suit and tie. Even old man Smithers was all decked out. We didn't even know they cared about Jimmy, yet they were both there. Many of the loggers from the lumberyard even made an appearance. News traveled fast; it always does in a small town. The service was nice and quick, lots of sobbing and tears from the crowd. The five of us guys gathered afterward, and we stared at each other, not knowing what to say. Everyone hovered around Jimmy's parents. Some of the mourners began to drift their way toward me for handshakes and awkward hugs.

Of course, the most devastated were Jimmy's parents. It was hard to look at them; making eye contact was impossible. I bowed my head when I shook their hands. Jimmy's mother pulled me in for a hug, which was very uncomfortable. No words could take away the pain or the emptiness that was in all of our hearts that day.

The local pastor said Jimmy was in a better place now. None of us kids could understand how that could be, especially if he wasn't hanging out with us. They say time heals all wounds; I sure hope so. I didn't think I could live with that kind of pain or emptiness forever.

A week had passed since that day. Late one evening, there came a knock at the front door. It was Jimmy's parents. They had put their home on the market and stopped in to say goodbye. They could no longer stay in the house where Jimmy once lived. It was time to move on, too many bad memories.

I remembered Father calling me downstairs. I didn't want to see his parents again. I knew it would hurt to much to face them. But they said they had something for me. Something that Jimmy wanted me to have. Curiosity won out.

"Hello," I greeted them, averting eye contact.

"Hi, Johnny," Jimmy's father whispered as he knelt down on one knee so he could look me in the eyes. "Thank you for being such a wonderful friend to our boy. You never knew how much you meant to him. He always thought the world of you. He never stopped talking about you. Even when you two managed to get into trouble, he still looked up to you." He whispered to me and then rubbed his hand on the top of my head, messing up my hair.

I cracked a little smile, trying to hide the pain I felt.

"We miss him, too," Jimmy's mother said in a soft voice. Her voice was almost peaceful and comforting, soothing to the soul. "We were cleaning out his things, boxing them up to give to needy families around the area. That's when we spotted this box in the back of his closet. A note was on the top of it with your name on it. I figured it was yours, or he wanted you to have it." I could hear her voice quiver as a tear ran down her cheek. Then she handed me a small, wooden box.

I thought back to that day on the creek when we stopped at Jimmy's house and how he took a long time upstairs. Did Jimmy know something was about to happen? I wiped a tear from my own cheek and rubbed my finger against the smooth wood. "Thank you," I whispered. An awful gnawing feeling grew in my gut. I could feel my face redden. I was embarrassed because I didn't know what else to say.

I stepped back and looked at the small wooden box. I turned and headed for the stairs. I stopped at the bottom and looked over my shoulder one last time at Jimmy's parents, giving them a wry grin before I made my way up the stairs. I stopped halfway, sat down, and gazed at the box. I felt horrible. I hadn't done enough that day. Jimmy was trying to tell me something that was going on his in life. Now, I was ashamed because I doubted him. I had thought it was one of his games.

I hadn't noticed Buck sitting at the top of the stairs. He stood and made his way down, pausing only for a second to lay a hand on my shoulder and pat me a few times. That was his way of saying everything was all right. "Sorry, bud, I miss him, too!" he confessed. Buck continued his way to the bottom of the stairs, stopped, turned to look at me again, and then disappeared. I heard him talking to Mr. and Mrs. Brooker.

I sat on the stairway and listened to all of them talk for several minutes. I looked up when Buck made his way back up the stairs. "Whatcha got there?" he asked, pointing to the small box that I gripped in my hands.

"Nothing."

"Well, it looks like something to me," he smiled as he reached out and tried to pull the box from my hands.

"Stop it!" I yelled, jumping to my feet and stomping up the stairs.

I was surprised when Buck didn't come after me, but I caught a glimpse of Father's head poking around the corner. Before I closed the door, I heard the low bass of my father's voice, "Show some respect, Buck. We have guests, and the box belongs to your brother."

I sat on the edge of my bed, alone, holding the box. I gazed at it and then turned it over and over in my hands. I thought it would be bigger. Jimmy had made it sound mysterious, full of magic or something mystical. I still didn't see why this box was so special. Minutes passed, maybe hours before fatigue finally won the battle, and I fell asleep, the box still in my hand.

When I woke, it was morning. I slowly made my way downstairs to get something to eat. That's when I spotted my favorite cereal on the table with a note attached from Mom. "Enjoy your Quisp, Love Mom." Quisp were crunchy little spaceships that tasted great. There was a small alien pictured on the box standing beside his spaceship. Yum, yum, good!

My mind kept racing back to the box Jimmy had left for me. *Was the box possessed? Did this box get Jimmy killed?* I shook my head. *That's impossible. I must be losing my mind. There is no way this box had anything to do with his death, and it couldn't contain any special powers. That was the stuff you only read about in books or saw at the picture show. Not something that happened in real life.*

I gazed out the front window of my bedroom toward the base of the mountain. Everything looked peaceful. The day passed by, and I did nothing but think about the box and Jimmy. Evening came quickly. I could see the fireflies sparkling outside in the twilight sky. The woods were alive and twinkling. A small smile crossed my face before I drifted off to sleep.

The next morning, I woke with a stiff neck. I was not surprised because I slept on the floor. I was still wearing the same clothes from the day before. I was holding the small wooden box firmly in my hand when a surprising knock came at the door. I didn't want to see anyone, but I called out, "Yeah?"

"Are you up?" Mother asked.

"Yeah, I'm up."

"You have a visitor. I'll send her up," she said.

A bit of panic set in. *"Her?"* I questioned.

I could hear light footsteps on the stairs as the person grew closer to the top. Then my visitor slowly pushed the door open.

"Johnny," the soft voice of a girl said when she poked her head around the corner.

I looked up and caught a gaze of Sara looking directly at me. A crooked smile had quirked my lips before it disappeared. Sara smiled back and took a few steps into my room before she stopped. "Hi," she said. The look on her face said it all, one of concern, someone who cared. "It's sad; I mean what happened to Jimmy." She fidgeted with her fingers before pushing her hair away from her face. "I'm so sorry for your loss."

"Thank you." I paused. "He was your friend, too," I mumbled. I noticed the kindness in her eyes and smile. I felt a warm fuzzy feeling growing inside. My heart stuttered, and my stomach started to churn. She had this way of putting a smile on my face. "I'm okay. I'm glad you're here," I blurted out. She reached out, laying her hand on top of mine. Her touch was soft and warm.

Her eyes blinked a few times, almost like she was flirting with me. She smiled, and I returned her smile. Our eyes made contact, holding the glance for what felt like an eternity. I was beginning to feel a little better, and I was happy that she stopped over. The sick, sinking feeling I had felt earlier appeared to fade, at least for now.

It had been several days since I had left my room other than to eat and use the bathroom. I wondered if she would notice that I hadn't been taking care of myself.

"What's that?" she asked, pointing at the small box tucked in my hand.

"It's a puzzle box, something Jimmy left for me."

144

"It looks really neat. Can I hold it?" she asked, holding out her hand expectantly.

I hesitated before placing the box in her outstretched hand. She smiled at me as she ran her fingers over the top, sides, and bottom of the box. Her eyes searched the box over and over. She seemed to be looking for something. "Does it open?" she asked.

"I don't know. I haven't tried." I frowned. *Does the box open, and if it does, what will I find inside?*

Chapter Fifteen

Sara and I spent hours trying to figure out how to open the puzzle box, even shaking it to see if anything would happen. It was a new challenge for both of us, something to distract our minds. Now we had a purpose, a new game that we both wanted to win.

Buck and Parker entered the room. "Ah, what do we have here?" Buck teased.

"It looks like a couple of lovebirds," Parker laughed at the two of us.

"Stop it, both of you," I yelled as I leaped to my feet, clenching my fists by my side. I was tired of them picking on Sara and me, and I wasn't going to put up with their attitudes any more.

"Or what?" Buck responded as he dropped his arms to his side and balled up his hands.

"Leave us alone," I barked, turned, and sat back down on the floor next to Sara. "We're busy, and we don't have time for you."

"What's that?" Buck asked, pointing to the box. He had only caught a glimpse of it the other day in the stairwell.

"It's a puzzle box, something Jimmy left for me."

"Let me see it," Parker said as he reached for the box.

I hesitated before turning the box over to him. He looked the box over, top to bottom, side to side. He showed it to Buck before he tossed it back to me.

"Be careful with that," I yelled back, shaking my head in disgust.

It was obvious they weren't going anywhere. So Sara and I decided to go to the attic and continue our work on the box. I opened the attic door. The stairwell was narrow and dark. As we made our way up the short flight of stairs, I tripped and stumbled, sending the box flying across the hard wooden floor. Both Sara and I scrambled to retrieve it, but it wasn't easy because the room was dark. I stood up reaching for the string, waving my hand in circles until I felt the twine between my fingers. I pulled the cord, and the light shined on the attic floor. That's when we noticed a small panel had opened on one side of the box. We sat in silence, our chins dropped as our eyes raced back and forth at each other then back to the box.

"Now what?" she asked.

I shrugged. "How should I know?"

My eyes blinked several times as I gazed at the box. Finally, after much delay, I reached over and picked it up, turned it over, and inspected it for any other clues. After careful examination, I decided to push on the open section. When I did, another piece of the box slid open. I looked over at Sara; her bright wide eyes mirrored my own. A light stream of mist began to emit from the opening, rising upward about a foot in the air. My heart raced, and I quickly pushed the open section closed and the outer panel as well.

"What'd you do that for?" Sara hissed. The tone of her voice was enough to let me know she wasn't very happy with me for closing the box.

"What did you want me to do?" I fired back. "We don't know what this is and... and I'm not sure I'm ready to find out just yet." The tension filled the air. "I need to do some research first; I'll look in the encyclopedia to see if I can learn anything about puzzle boxes."

The tension broke when a loud knock at the door startled us both. For a few seconds, we just looked at one another, and then began to laugh.

"Who's there?" I chuckled.

"Johnny, will you come downstairs please? You have a visitor," Father announced.

Completely puzzled, I slowly stood up and made my way to the door. "Wait here. I'll be back," I said.

I left the attic, walked across the bedroom, and made my way down the stairs. The entire time I wondered who it could be. If it were Scooter or Todd, Father would have just sent them up. So that ruled those two out, and it dang sure wasn't Jimmy. I placed one foot after the other until I reached the bottom of the stairs. My mind raced with anticipation. Then I heard a man's voice talking to my father. I fell short of breath and froze a few steps from the bottom. *Oh no, it's the cops! That's the last thing I need, to answer a bunch of dumb questions about the accident.*

Then I thought I recognized the voice. So that ruled out the police; the voice was familiar, but I couldn't put a name to it. I took the final step then slowly turned the corner to see who was talking. Much to my surprise, it was Tom Evans, the owner of the general store. A sick feeling rushed over me. *Oh no! He's here to rat me out, telling Father that Buck and I had done something wrong at the store.*

"Hi, Johnny," Mr. Evans said, reaching out his hand in a friendly gesture.

"Hi, Mr. Evans," I reluctantly replied and slowly extended my hand to meet his. As we shook hands, Father motioned for all of us to take a seat.

"I'm very sorry for the loss of your friend. If there's anything I can do to help, please let me know."

I knew he didn't stop by to say he was sorry for the loss of my friend. "Thank you," I took a deep breath. "I'm sure that's not the reason you stopped by, is it? So how can I help you, Mr. Evans?"

"Johnny!" Father barked loudly. "Where are your manners?"

"That's okay." Tom raised his hand, motioning to my father. "Your son's a smart boy, and he's right. I didn't stop just for that reason." Tom's gaze was fixed on my eyes. I squirmed under the weight of his stare. "As you know, Jimmy worked for me at the store. He came by almost every day after school. He even spent an hour or two a day working during the summer months, stocking shelves, sweeping, taking out the trash, things like that. I could use some help, and I wondered if you would be interested in the job. I'll pay you like I paid Jimmy—a dollar a day if that's good with you." He paused, his eyes never leaving mine. "I don't need an answer today. Take your time, think it over, and let me know tomorrow." He stood, shook my hand and then Father's, and thanked us for our time before saying goodbye. "See you tomorrow," he smiled.

I stood, not quite sure what to make of Mr. Evans' offer; I felt more skeptical than anything. *Mr. Evans must want something. Could he know that Jimmy had given me the puzzle box? That would explain it; he wanted the box back.* I bolted toward the attic stairs to share the news with Sara.

She sat at the top of the bedroom stairs. She had eavesdropped on the entire conversation. "You can't work for him," she said rudely.

"Wow, that's harsh, don't ya think?" I sneered.

"I'm sorry, but he gives me the creeps."

Ignoring her comment, I said, "He offered me a job working at the store, cleaning up and stuff like that."

"You're not going to take it, are you?" Concern shot over her face.

"Yeah, why not?"

"I can tell you why not. I don't trust him. He's up to something."

"I understand your concern, but what better way to learn what he's up too than by working for him, right?" I was hatching a plan, maybe not a good one, but it was the best I could come up with in a short amount of time. "I'm going to take the job," I told her.

Her eyes downcast, she frowned. "Is there anything I could say that would talk you out of taking the job?"

"Nope, I've already made up my mind."

She sighed. "Then, please, be careful."

Later that evening, I lay in bed reading the encyclopedia. There was a lot of information about ghosts and the supernatural. Some of it was a little hard to believe, but so was seeing a ghost. After what happened to Jimmy, I was open to anything. The book stated that to become a ghost, you would have to die before your time, either murdered or by accident. Those ghosts would be stuck haunting this world until the one thing that was keeping them here was solved, releasing them to the other side. But in the case of suicide, they were damned to walk this world for all eternity. *So Annabelle wasn't going anywhere as long as Parker's story was true.* I thought as I continued to read.

Ghosts can make themselves appear to mortals, but only if they choose. Maybe that's why Jimmy could see her, and I couldn't. What I found most fascinating was that ghosts can haunt only an area where they once lived or visited. That explained why Annabelle could move around so much. She had been all over these woods when she was alive.

Ghosts can't physically hurt mortals. That was good news. But they can suggest you do something you normally would not, something that could result in injury or even death! I thought about how Jimmy appeared to be in a trance in those final moments. Had she been controlling him?

What if there was more than one ghost, possibly two, maybe even three if you think about the old man? I quickly realized that Annabelle's young lover could cross over if what linked him to this world was solved. *So what was keeping him here? We knew who killed him. But why hadn't he crossed over? Or had he crossed over and was she searching for nothing, maybe just revenge because she was alone? And whatever happened to Annabelle's real husband? Where was he? Or was he the one behind all of the hauntings?*

Something inside told me the answer could be in the puzzle box. Tossing down the 'G' encyclopedia, I picked up the one starting with 'P.' Flipping through the pages, I reached the section labeled 'PU,' puzzle boxes. There it was: everything you wanted to know about puzzle boxes. I didn't care when they began or who made them. I only wanted to know what was inside. I quickly learned that various things could be in the puzzle box, from keys to riddles; some could even be enchanted, depending on where the box came from and how old it was.

My interest was piqued even more. Maybe Tom knew more than he shared with Jimmy. That was obvious and led me back to the thought of working for Mr. Evans. I wondered if that was the right thing to do. I thought about the pros and cons. *It would give me a chance to learn more about the box and the old legends. Maybe I would even learn more about Jimmy since he and Tom had spent so much time together.*

Another thought raced through my mind: Why didn't Jimmy ever tell me that he had a job? I always thought Jimmy needed to go home to help his mother after school. On the downside, what if Mr. Evans was evil? What if he was the one who put Jimmy under a spell? My mind whirled back to the day I saw his dark eyes in the store. That thought sent goose bumps racing down my spine.

That night I tossed and turned, unable to sleep. I had too many thoughts in my head. I couldn't wait until morning so that I could visit Mr. Evans' and find out if my fears were true or not.

Soon, the sun began peeking through the curtains. The morning had come at last. A little tired from the restless night, I crept out of bed. Slowly, I put on my clothes and carried my shoes down the stairs, not wanting to wake up Buck. I had no time to explain why I was leaving so early in the morning.

I rounded the corner and made my way to the kitchen. "You're up early."

Startled, I took a step back. "Hi Dad. You scared me. I didn't expect anyone up this early."

"I'm just getting ready for work. I'll be out of here in a minute. Oh, by the way, did you think about Mr. Evans' offer?"

"I sure did."

"Well? Are you going to tell me?"

"Sorry, Dad, yes," I answered.

"Yes, what? Yes, you're going to tell me, or yes, you're going to take the job?" Father was getting a little annoyed with my evasive answers.

"I'm sorry. Yes, I'm going to take the job." I smiled.

"Great, I'm proud of you. Glad you're going to get out of the house and earn a little money. Well, I'd better hit the road, or I'm going to be late. Tell me all about your first day when I get home."

"Sure will, Dad. Have a good day. Bye." I sighed in relief as I watched Father drive off.

I polished off my bowl of Quisp cereal before making my way out the front door. I grabbed my bicycle and peddled toward the dam. The quick trip ended with me purposely skidding sideways. I liked to watch the pebbles fly as I brought my bike to stop. I took a deep breath, and the smell of fresh dust filled my nose.

The wet morning dew covered the plants. As I watched the steam rise upward from the creek, my mind began wandering; I looked left and then right. The sound of the water pouring over the spillway roared. I had never thought much about it until now, but the water never stopped. Always flowing. So where did it all come from? It never seemed to end. It had the power to move large objects, even take a life. I sat there for a few minutes in silence, watching the world wake up. The trees and wildlife, everything was rising to what was going to be a wonderful day. The sun peeked over the top of the mountain, and the warmth beating down on me sent a smile to my face.

It was time to ride. Pushing the pedal down, I sped down the dirt path that followed the water's edge. I thought back to the times when Jimmy and I rode these trails. Faster and faster I went around many tight corners. I broke to the left and then back to the right, kicking up the dirt in my wake. I was in the groove. I felt like I was racing in motocross, a man with no fear, a Wildman like Jimmy. I pushed myself faster and quickly made my way along the two-mile stretch that brought me out at the base of the bridge. After arriving, I paused to reflect. *This ride was for you, my friend.* I smiled and began to push my bike up the steep embankment. Slowly, I lifted it over the metal guardrails before placing it firmly on old Lizardville Road.

With Salona only a half mile farther from where I sat, I pushed off and headed to the general store. I finally felt like my old self—refreshed and with a purpose. Everything was going my way. Life was good.

Pushing the back peddle downward with my foot, I engaged the brakes, causing the bike to slide on the pavement before coming to a stop. As I placed my foot down firmly on the ground, I looked over my shoulder to admire the five-foot black rubber mark I left on the surface. Looking forward, I noticed the general store some twenty feet away. Feeling confident, I coasted toward the store. It was time to face the demons.

Chapter Sixteen

I coasted my bike to the back of the store and glanced around a bit before laying it on the ground next to the building. I strode to the front, stopping at the corner where I paused to take a look around. *No crows*, I turned and marched the final steps before pushing the door open to the sound of ringing bells that hung over it.

Mr. Evans quietly came out of the back room. No funny smell hung in the air this morning. His face lit up with delight. I could tell he was glad to see me. "Well, good morning, Johnny!"

"Hello, Mr. Evans."

"Oh please, just call me Tom." He laughed. "I hope you're here to tell me you'll accept my offer." He raised his eyebrows and waited for my response.

"I am," I paused. "Yes, I would like to work here. And thank you."

"I'm pleased," Tom said and smiled at me. "Let me show you around. Then I'll tell you what I need to have done today so you can get to work." He was excited I had said yes. That made me feel better. Maybe I was wrong about Mr. Evans.

The store was bigger than it looked and busier than I thought. Between selling gas and groceries, the place seemed to be hopping. I worked on sweeping floors, breaking down the cardboard boxes, and stacking them out back. Tom showed me how to restock some shelves. Later, I would gather and dispose of all the garbage, separating the burnable items from the non-burnable items. There was a small burning pit out back near the edge of the woods that Tom told me we would use later that evening. I stayed busy, and the time passed quickly.

After working in the store a few weeks, Tom surprised me one evening and asked if I could stay for dinner. I didn't see why not, so he called my parents to let them know.

"What are you hungry for?" Tom asked and handed me a Pepsi.

I smiled and took a long sip. "Thanks."

Tom nodded. "I can throw a few hot dogs on the grill out back if you like."

"Sure," I smiled. I loved hot dogs smothered in ketchup. Some folks preferred mustard, but not me; I'm a ketchup kind of guy.

Tom locked the door and turned the *closed* sign around in the window before making his way to the cooler where he grabbed a pack of hotdogs and headed for the back door. "How many would you like?"

"Two would be nice, Mr. Evans."

"I told you; call me Tom."

"Got it."

The smell of roasting hot dogs filled the air. I took a deep breath trying to inhale the aroma. "Aah," I sighed. "I love summer and barbecues."

In no time at all, the dogs were ready, and the two of us sat out back eating and swapping stories. If you didn't know it, you would think we had been friends forever. I grabbed another Pepsi from the cooler. This pleased Tom. He could tell I was feeling comfortable in the store and around him. I guess that's why he felt the time was right to share something with me.

"Johnny, I'd like to talk to you about something, if I may." He paused, searching to find the right words. "I know you miss Jimmy." Tom looked at me with a sympathetic look. "Me, too. His loss was devastating for all of us." He averted his eyes to the woods. "I want to talk to you about the box Jimmy gave you." I quickly perked up. *Bingo*. "I gave it to him to see if he could figure out how to open it. I never meant for him to keep the box or give it away." He frowned. "You see, the box was passed down to me by my mother. She told me one of our ancient relatives had placed something special in the box. Some family secret, I suppose. To be honest, I don't know what it contains. I just know it's been in my family a very long time. Almost a hundred years. That's why I'm asking for it back."

Before my lips could move, he continued. "I know his parents gave you the box. They told me so before they moved away," he said, staring directly into my eyes as he fumbled with his hands.

"You're asking me to give the box back to you?" I sounded shocked. I was playing things up a bit.

"If you don't mind, that would be nice if you returned it back to its rightful owner." I felt like Tom was trying to make me feel a little guilty for holding on to it.

"So, you've never opened the box?" I asked, changing the subject.

"No, I've never opened the box. That's why I asked for Jimmy's help. It's not broken, is it?" Tom asked studying my face trying to determine if I had figured out how to open it.

"No, it's not damaged. I just wondered if it opened; most boxes do." I answered with a wry smile.

"Oh, I suppose it does open. It's just old and fragile," he said, sounding a little disappointed. "Please think about bringing the box back. If you don't, that's okay, too." I could hear the hint of sarcasm in his voice. He was obviously trying to keep me at bay.

"I don't want to be rude, but can I think about it a little while?"

He nodded, letting me know that was fine. The two of us finished our meal, cleaned up, and then reopened the store. I was getting ready to leave when old man Smithers stopped for gas and a loaf of bread. He grumbled at Tom and pointed toward me. I tried to listen, but I couldn't make out the words the two men were saying. I had this burning feeling that old man Smithers was complaining about me working at the store. Tom seemed to smile and just listen. I didn't want to lose the job after just a few weeks. After all, I thought I was doing a pretty good job, and the extra money came in handy.

A half hour had passed before Tom told me I better head home and handed me another Pepsi for the ride. "See you tomorrow, and please bring the bottle back," he instructed. I took a swig and peddled off toward the house.

When I returned home, I was surprised to learn my parents were out running errands. With them out of the way, I wasted no time grabbing the phone and calling everyone to come over. I assured them it was extremely important. I decided it was time to bring everyone up to speed, including telling them the stories that Jimmy shared with me. It didn't take long before Parker and his sisters arrived. They joined Buck, who was sitting at the kitchen table stuffing food in his face. None of them understood what was so important that they needed to drop everything and rush over for a special meeting or why it had to be this late in the evening.

A loud knock at the front door startled the gang. Only I remained calm and proceeded to open it. Scooter and Todd had arrived.

"What's so important that it couldn't wait until morning?" blurted Scooter.

"Yeah, what gives, man?" inquired Todd.

"Come on in so we can get started," I said, pointing toward the kitchen. I stepped aside allowing them to pass and make their way toward the kitchen.

"I'm sure you're all wondering why I asked you here. Well, with my folks out of the house, I couldn't think of a better time." I glanced around the room at all the puzzled faces.

"Before Jimmy passed away..." I felt my voice falter, so I cleared my throat and continued, "he shared something with me. He said Annabelle had paid him a few visits." Then I told them every story Jimmy told me. The room erupted with doubters. I wasn't expecting that. I had thought they would be more open. Lexi remained calm, reached out to the others asking for silence, and nodded for me to go ahead. "I didn't believe him either, not at first. Too many things have happened, and now he's gone. He told me she was looking for a puzzle box, the box that his parents gave me." Their eyes grew wide.

"Tom gave the box to Jimmy, with the hope that he could figure out how to open it. Unfortunately, he never did, just like Tom never did. Then, Jimmy's parents stopped by a week after he passed and left the box with me, saying Jimmy wanted me to have it."

"I remember that night," Buck blurted out. "Ah, sorry, go ahead," he motioned me on.

"Once Mr. Evans found out I possessed the box, he offered me a job working at the store, one that I graciously accepted." A few whispers between the others and then I held up my hands asking for silence. "First, I could use the extra cash, and second, I wanted to know more about this box. I've been very patient, but today at the store, Tom inquired about the box and asked if he could have it back. He informed me it was a family heirloom. I told him I would think it over. He was fine with that, but before I do anything, I wanted to get your thoughts on whether I should give him the box back or if I should try to open it again."

A nervous rumbling broke out as they all tried to talk at once. Buck motioned for everyone to stop and said "Wait, wait, just a minute." He questioned, a bit baffled, "What do you mean, open it again?" His eyes fixed on mine.

"Have you already opened the box? What's inside?" asked Parker excitedly.

"No, no, I haven't opened it. That was a slip of the tongue," I stammered.

"That's not true," Sara whimpered and immediately covered her mouth. "Sorry Johnny." She frowned and bowed her head.

"Okay, okay, I accidentally opened the box," I confessed, backing away from the table. The others talked amongst themselves, whispering so I couldn't hear. Sara made her way around the table to me. Laying her hand on my arm, she told me she was sorry for her slip of the tongue. "The words just slipped out my mouth," she pleaded. I nodded, letting her know that everything was fine. It was bound to come out sometime.

An eerie silence fell over the room. "Can we see the box again?" asked Parker.

"Sure… I guess. It's upstairs." I sighed with a little hesitation. "Just remember it's my box. It was left to me." I looked around to make sure everyone agreed.

Motioning for them to follow, I made my way to the stairs that led to the bedroom Buck and I shared. "Please ignore the mess; Buck doesn't know how to clean up after himself." The words were barely out of my mouth before I felt the sharp pain of Bucks fist slam into my arm. "Ouch," I wailed and flashed a nasty look at Buck.

Once we were all in the room, I wedged open the attic door. The creaking sounds of the old boards wailed under the pounding feet as each of us climbed the steep, narrow entrance.

The attic was dark and hot, and the air stagnant due to lack of circulation. A musky smell loomed in the large room. Dust covered boxes stacked along the walls stretched to the ceiling. An old rocking chair covered in plastic sat in the corner. A thick layer of dust covered that. One by one, we entered. I felt around trying to find the string to pull. Once I had the light on, I motioned for each of them to sit on the floor.

We gathered in a small circle: Buck, Lexi, and Parker, followed by Sara and Todd, who sat on the opposite side. Scooter took the last remaining spot next to Todd, leaving just one place for me.

I walked toward the old hope chest on the far side of the room and opened it slowly. It had belonged to my grandmother before she passed away. I propped open the lid, moved a few blankets, and laid them to the side.

I grabbed a small stack of old newspapers. Gram loved rereading the important events that happened in her life. I looked at a few; the front page of one read, "The Johnstown Flood." *Wow, that was 1936.* The Cuban missile crisis and "President Kennedy Shot" splashed across other pages in large bold print. Her entire life was now collecting dust, stored in this large wooden chest in our attic. I paused for a second to reflect. *Would this be my life one day, just a box of memories sitting in an attic?*

Curious, the group waited, the suspense killing them. They began looking back and forth at each other, waiting to get a look at this mysterious box.

"Hey, did you get lost over there?" shouted Buck.

"Sorry, I'll be there in a second," I said, gently placing the newspapers to the side before picking up the small wooden box that held the key to who knows what. I stood and turned to face the others, holding the box for all to see.

A few oohs and aahs came from the group before the laughter broke out. "You called us all here to look at that little box?" Parker complained, rolling his eyes.

"You had better not waste our time," roared Buck.

"Relax guys," Lexi interrupted. "I want to see the box, please." Extending her hand, she gazed at me with gentle eyes.

I hesitated before handing the box over to Lexi. She rolled it over and over again looking at all sides. She felt every smooth edge of its surface. Gliding her long fingers over the top and around the sides, she worked her way to the bottom before handing the box over to Buck.

Buck looked at the box briefly and quickly tossed it to Parker as if he were not impressed. Parker took the box and handed it over to Todd without even as much as a glance. Todd gazed at the box briefly. Then he tried to push on the sides and the top, but nothing happened. "My Aunt Carolyn in New

Orleans would know all about this box. It's probably some voodoo box that contains special powers," he stated.

"Are you kidding me?" blurted Parker. "I'm out of here. What a waste of time. I could be home watching American Bandstand." He shoved himself up and threw a dirty look my way.

"Wait," Sara said. "Don't you want to see what happens when it opens?" she asked, making eye contact with her brother and pleading for him to give it a chance.

Parker nodded and glanced back at me. "All right, dork, open the box." Then he sat Indian style on the floor.

Todd handed the box back to me. Sara nodded her head and smiled at me, trying to reassure me that everything would be fine. I took my spot on the floor beside the others. I nervously looked at each of my friends and swallowed hard. I fixed my eyes on the box. Frightened, I pushed on the top section, but nothing happened. I glanced across the circle at Sara with a look of confusion. I pushed and then pulled again on the top of the box to no avail.

Disappointment quickly set in. Parker and Buck were ready to bolt for the attic stairs. Todd waved his arm, motioning for them to sit. Scooter sat quietly, patiently waiting for something to happen, anything.

Sara motioned with her hand for me to toss the box on the floor. I was a bit puzzled, but I quickly realized that was how the box opened the first time. Holding the box flat in my hand, I lightly tossed it to floor where it landed in the center of the circle. Nothing happened!

We all gazed at the box, waiting for a sign of life, but there was no movement, nothing at all. Desperately, I lunged forward, picked the box up, this time tossing it harder end-over-end to the middle of the circle. The box rolled over and over, like the first time when it opened. It came to a sudden stop when the top lid slid open.

* * *

"This story is getting a little farfetched, don't you think?" Zack smiled at me.

The thunder continued to roar outside. A bright flash followed by another loud crack and more rumbling as I watched the candlelight flicker.

"Not at all. You wanted me to share my childhood stories with you, so I am." I gazed at them.

"I think you're making this stuff up as you go along," Daniel chimed, casting a look at my eyes and trying to determine if I was lying.

"I'm getting older, so my memory isn't what it used to be," I explained.

"Whatever, dude," said Zack.

"I think you're trying to scare us, aren't you?" Daniel added.

"Not at all."

"Are you going to continue?" Daniel searched for answers and then shrugged his shoulders.

"Sure." I was enjoying spending some one on one time with my boys.

Chapter Seventeen

The box lay in the center of the circle with the top lid open. Buck, Parker, and the others sat quietly waiting for something magical to happen. I felt justification as I fumbled my way to the middle before picking it up. The others looked on as I moved the second panel and revealed another section of the box.

What happened next was amazing. A soft blue-white light emitted from the center of the box. I laid the box back onto the floor. The mist slowly began to rise upward. I looked at it and then glanced at the others. Buck had the "deer in the headlights" thing going on. Parker was fascinated, to say the least, and leaned forward to get a better look. I could tell the box had piqued Lexi's interest; her eyes grew wide. Todd sat, slowly moving his head from side to side, trying to get a better view. Sara looked on with justification beaming from her smile, silencing all the doubters. Scooter's face was white, like he had seen a ghost.

I felt a tingly feeling rushing up from the tips of my toes all the way up my spine. Goose bumps broke out on my arms, and I shivered from head to toe. The cloudy substance continued to ooze from the box. Continuing to grow, the mist rose to a foot tall before spreading out.

Buck started to scoot backward a bit. Lexi reached and placed her hand on his arm. She gazed at him and shot him a saucy smile, briefly stealing his heart. I witnessed the powerful pull Lexi had over him, which is what convinced Buck to stay.

"This gives me the willies," whispered Parker, being the first to break the silence.

"Where's the mist coming from?" Lexi questioned.

I extended my arm forward and grabbed the box, sliding one section closed and then another. "Sorry, guys; this freaks me out." The mist dissipated into thin air.

"That's it? You just closed the box?" Lexi hissed.

"I... I don't know," I said with a sigh.

"We need to find out what's in the box, if anything," Lexi argued to the group. She glanced over to Todd. He nodded back, the excitement shining in his eyes. Lexi looked to Buck, who nodded back, and then Parker, Scooter, Sara, and lastly, me.

"So, we're all in?" Lexi paused then continued, "This is for Jimmy."

"Should we take some precautions?" I asked nervously.

"Against what?" barked Todd. "Crickets, spiders, maybe ghosts?"

None of us had any idea what the box contained. The only way to find out was to open it and let it do its thing, if it even did anything more than emit a mist. *Maybe the spell wore out over time, and all that was left was a cloudy mist.*

"So we're all in agreement?" asked Lexi again, and we all silently nodded. "Great, now open the damn box." She glared at me.

I held the box in my hand and turned it over and over again before I tossed it back onto the floor. The box rolled end over end, and the top section slid open. I moved forward, picking it up and, once again, sliding the second panel open before I laid it back on the floor. The mist almost immediately began to rise. The small cloud formed over the box. Much to our surprise, the box leaped up a few inches from the floor as another section sprang open. We all simultaneously jumped with the box's movement. The mist quickly began to escape the newly opened section and formed a large cloud directly over the container.

Wide-eyed and shocked, we all sat amazed, speechless, as the mist continued to grow before our eyes, forming a large four to five-foot diameter cloud. Inside the mist, something began to happen. Strands of mist started changing colors, gathering together, and intertwining and making something before our eyes. The figures danced, leaped back and forth, and glistened in the mist.

Still paralyzed on the attic floor, we sat in a circle surrounding the large pocket of mist. The movement of the swirling patterns inside mesmerized us. One by one, we began to notice something taking shape. Slowly a picture was developing in the middle of the formation. A vision of a landscape, taking the shape of trees and rocks, with a sprinkle of bushes and a dirt trail. A small creek trickling down a mountainside led to a slender waterfall cascading over the face of a cliff and splashing into a little pool of water at the base. The image continued to grow, becoming brighter, clearer, and more defined.

"It looks like a trail in the woods. It could be the one behind our house," Parker hinted.

"I recognize the waterfall," Lexi whispered.

"Yeah, you're right; I know where that's at," Buck said with a hint of excitement in his voice. "It's a map!"

The vision had cleared, becoming more visible by the second. Parker, Buck, and Lexi had spent more time in the woods than the rest of us. They were the first to recognize the image. The dirt path lead to a waterfall located a few miles behind the Parker's home, close to the top of the mountain.

"This makes sense," Parker said, grinning with excitement. "The path leads to the waterfall, and the dark hole could be a cave entrance located behind it, or it's close to the falls."

"Okay, why the vision?" Lexi paused. "Why a waterfall and a cave? Is the box trying to tell us something?" Lexi analyzed it and then us, her question hanging in the air.

"It all makes sense. Don't you see the path, the waterfall, even the cave? If it's in the woods behind your home," I pointed to Parker and his sisters, "then the box is giving us clues where to find something," I surmised, my eyes growing wider with the realization.

"What makes sense?" pleaded Todd.

"Remember, guys? This box is a family heirloom that was passed down for many years. It belongs to Mr. Evans, the general store owner. He gave Jimmy the box to see if he could open it. When Jimmy passed away, the box was left to me. Don't you see?" By the look on their faces, they still didn't get it. I was getting a bit frustrated. "Okay, let me back up. Think about the ghost story Parker told us a few weeks back, the night we all camped out, the story about Annabelle and her lover, who was killed by the old man." One by one, their eyes sparkled with understanding. "In the end, she hung herself, and after her death, none of the bodies were every found. Do you see now? The box is leading us to the bodies!" Enthusiasm laced my voice as I finally unlocked the final piece to the mystery.

The temperature quickly dropped, sending a chill in the air. A light breeze blew inside the closed room. The bright flash of a light dashed across the room, blurring the cloud of mist that floated before us.

Startled, we all cowered closer to the floor. The cloudy white figure danced back and forth a few times until the image became distorted.

A loud screeching sound echoed in the attic. Lexi and the rest of us covered our ears. The sound was so loud that it hurt my head. I had never heard anything quite like it. The light flickered a time or two, right before the bulb popped. I was cursing under my breath. Why had we opened this box? I grew frantic and then found something inside of me I didn't know I had. Courage.

"STOP IT," I yelled. "You can't hurt us! I'm not afraid of you! I'm not afraid! I'm not afraid!" I repeated the chant several times.

The deafening sound ceased, and the temperature returned to normal. Even the wind died down. "What just happened?" Lexi wondered.

There was no logical answer. I remained calm as I watched the others suffer panic attacks.

"I can't do this," Todd whined, shaking his head and showing no signs of approval. "This is something my Aunt Carolyn would like, but not me. I'm out."

Parker shrugged his shoulders, not knowing what to believe. "Was that a ghost?" he asked. He looked a little pale, and the look on his face told me he agreed with my theory. "The stories have to be true," he whispered.

Lexi's fascination grew; she enjoyed reading about the paranormal, and now was her chance to find out if it was more than just a myth. "I wanna go to the woods," she sang. "I need to see what's out there."

"I can't let you go alone," Buck chimed in, trying to put on a brave front.

A little excited, I asked, "So what's next?"

Sara nodded in approval. She later told me that she had wanted to be brave for me, even if it meant coming face to face with a ghost. None of us knew what lurked by the falls.

"I think we need to check it out," said Parker.

"Are you all nuts?" Todd asked, raising his hands in front of him. "This is crazy shit. You have no idea what you're about to find, and what if it's dangerous? Did you all just see that thing?"

I quickly replied. "We'll be fine. I've done some research on ghosts, and they can't harm us. I promise. Didn't you see how I cast that one out of the room?"

"Yeah, but…" I think Todd was about to change his mind before he was interrupted.

"I'll go," Scooter said quietly, sitting in the dark. A ray of light cast over his face. The only light in the room came from the ventilation fan on the far wall. He took a deep breath. "This is for Jimmy, but if we find the cave, I'm not going in. I don't like the dark. Now, can we get out of here?"

Scooter wanted to go; now that shocked everyone. Todd nodded his head and agreed to go along with no guarantee he was going inside the cave. That's if we even found one.

"No one's going make you go in the cave if you don't want to," said Parker.

"Yeah, just like you weren't going to make him jump off the bridge either," I sarcastically replied.

"Let it go, will you? I give you my word," Parker replied, laying his hand on his heart.

"Is everyone okay with meeting at our house tomorrow morning? Say about nine?" Lexi asked.

We all nodded. I leaned forward toward the box. I waved my hand directly through what remained of the mist, sending ripples from the bottom upward to the top. It reminded me of a rock plunging into the water. I watched the waves rolling outward. The mist felt cold on my hands as I rubbed my fingers together.

I wanted to learn more about the box. How could it reflect an image in the air? What made the mist? Where'd it come from? However, considering the circumstances, I knew these questions would have to wait. The others were already making their way out of the attic.

I gently laid my hands on the box, picked it up, and closed the top section. The cloud started to fade. The size of the cloud dramatically shrank as I closed up the next section. Soon, the entire cloud would be gone as I closed the third and final panel.

One by one, we made our way out of the attic and gathered downstairs in the family room. The seven of us were fascinated with the image the box displayed; a few talked about the ghost or what we thought might have been a ghost. But we never stopped to think that the box had already taken one life and could very easily take another.

Chapter Eighteen

Another sleepless night for me, but this time, I wasn't the only one who tossed and turned. I could tell Buck was struggling to sleep. The hours passed slowly before the sun shone through the thin curtains. Morning, at last. I bounced out of bed full of excitement and as refreshed as one could be for a sleepless night. Buck wasn't far behind. We packed a few things, including two flashlights and the puzzle box, into a small backpack before making our way to the Parker residence.

They were all gathered in the family room. Buck and I were the last to arrive. A few were still talking about the vision the box had shown; Lexi complained it was too early in the morning, and she needed more sleep. The consensus was that time was a-wasting, and we needed to hit the trail so we could solve this mystery.

Buck informed Parker that we had brought two flashlights and the puzzle box. Parker said they had some flashlights in the kitchen, and he dashed over to grab them.

"Do you think we should fill a canteen or two just in case?" I asked.

"Not a bad idea." Buck laughed, placing me in a headlock and rubbing his fist over the top of my head. "That's my little brother, always thinking of everything." Buck watched Lexi sway her way to the kitchen to fill the canteens.

"Stop it," I squealed, trying to pull away from Buck.

The crew looked around one last time. Lexi returned from the kitchen with two canteens full of water. Parker and Buck looked over the supplies. Four working flashlights, three extra D-cell batteries, two canteens full of water, and one puzzle box, nicely tucked in the small backpack.

We made our way to the front door. Buck paused and glanced back at the rest of us. "Last chance to change your mind," he warned. After no response, he wrapped his hand around the knob, turned it clockwise, and pulled the door open.

"Well, hello. I was just about to knock," Mr. Evans blurted out, blocking our exit.

"What the hell!" Buck yelled jumping back and bumping into Lexi, forcing her into Parker. We looked like a row of dominos toppling as the seven of us began to stumble backward one at a time.

"Where are you off to so early in the morning?" Mr. Evans asked in his masculine voice.

Regaining his balance, Buck snapped, "None of your business."

Parker jumped forward, standing directly beside Buck. Todd moved forward, taking his spot beside Parker to form a single united front. I could see Mr. Evans looked a little awkward; maybe he was surprised by their actions. I wondered if he could tell that we were up to something. He tilted his head to the side and noticed the small backpack I was carrying along with the canteens. "I stopped to see if Johnny was here. Your parents said you were," Mr. Evans admitted as he looked past the three.

"I'm here," I muttered and stepped forward.

"Would you be able to work tomorrow, say around noon?" he asked.

I was caught off guard a little. *Why didn't he tell me that yesterday?* "Ah, sure, I'll see you at noon."

"Great, I'll see you then." He smiled, turned, and strolled to his car.

"I have this strange feeling. He's up to something," Buck said as he closed the door behind him.

We watched Mr. Evans drive off in the opposite direction of the general store. Then, we waited a few more minutes to make sure he didn't double back. We all found it a little odd that he stopped just to ask if I could work tomorrow. After several minutes of waiting, we decided it was safe to leave.

One by one, the seven of us made our way back to the door. Several things crossed my mind. I wondered how the box could cast a vision in the air, which could lead to a cave located behind the falls. And what if we found the cave, then what? Should we explore it? I wondered what we'd find once we were inside.

I was deep in my thoughts until Sara nudged me, bringing me back to reality.

"Do you think Mr. Evans will follow us?" inquired Todd.

"I don't think so. Why would he?" replied Buck.

"I don't trust him; he's a creepy old man," Sara snarled.

"I don't know why you even work for him. He makes me nervous," Lexi mentioned as her upper lip curled into a sneer.

"Stop! Stop!" Parker shouted. "Let's go out the basement, just to be sure he doesn't follow us." That sounded like a great idea, so we all turned and silently followed Parker downstairs, like ducklings following their mother, and waited by the back door. "Last chance to back out," Parker said as he made eye contact with each of us.

Lexi, Buck, and Todd nodded; Sara held onto my arm, and we both nodded. Scooter, wide-eyed as he swallowed, shrugged his shoulders to signal yes. It was obvious none of us were changing our minds. I guess curiosity had taken over.

"Great," Parker said, opening the basement door. The morning dew sat fresh on the lawn, showing our footprints as we made our way to the small dirt path that would take us deep into the woods.

The path quickly narrowed, forcing us to walk in single file. Buck walked closely behind Lexi, no doubt noticing how tight her jeans were that day. His head bobbed from side to side in stride with every step she took. I nodded to Scooter and pointed toward Buck. We both snickered a bit, thinking Buck must have a bad crush on Lexi. It didn't take long before the others noticed, too. Sara whispered something to Lexi, who glanced over her shoulder and gave Buck one of her saucy smiles, and then winked to let him know she approved of his actions.

Onward and upward, we trudged, deeper and deeper into the woods. Thirty minutes into our trip, Lexi whined that she needed a break. The steady incline had begun to wear on her.

We stopped and took a spot on a large boulder near the path and waited as she tried to catch her breath. We passed the canteen around so everyone could take a few sips. For me, I just wanted to get to the top. I was anxious to see what we might find.

The leaves began to rustle, as a cool breeze swept across the path. The wind whirled; maybe the mountain was trying to send a message to us. In the distance, I could hear some crows squawking.

"How weird was that?" Parker mentioned just as the wind began to die down. Buck agreed with a nod of his head. It was time to move on.

Another thirty minutes passed, and we drew closer to the top of the ridge just shy of the last tall peak. I noticed a small stream flowing across the path. It was barely a foot wide and went undetected by most of our group as they stepped over. Then it vanished down the slope. We walked a little farther up the ridge before the path wound back around toward the little stream.

We continued to trudge on. The path narrowed once again, allowing only single file passage. Thick foliage covered many areas, and the branches raked across our arms as we pushed our way through. I could tell this was a path that hunters used. The forest had grown over it since hunting season was over.

The small brush that lay over our path hid sharp edged rocks that protruded from the ground. The rough terrain was making travel hard, and we began to slow. The steep incline had Todd complaining about the thinning air making it hard to breathe.

We laughed, telling him we were only a little over two thousand feet up.

"Hold on. Just a few more minutes and we'll be at the top," Parker announced.

"Quiet," I yelled and came to a stop. We stood in silence for a few moments; we could hear the faint sound of water smashing into a pool of water in the near distance. I looked around and noticed the smiles on everyone's faces. I think we all came to the same conclusion: we were close.

That path completely disappeared. Parker used his feet and the large walking stick he carried to clear a path large enough for us to make our way through the thick brush. The sound of the splashing water grew as we closed in on the base of the falls.

The trees were rustling. *Were they whispering to each other?* We made our way through the thick foliage one step at a time. I wondered if the trees were sharing secrets, or possibly warning the cave as we approached. An eerie feeling rushed over me when we arrived at the base of the hidden falls.

The splashing water was almost on top of us. Parker broke off a few more branches that revealed the small pond at the base of the waterfall. The water was clean and crystal clear. It made a great place to top off the canteens. The pond itself was only a foot or two deep and maybe ten feet in diameter.

A three-foot wide thin layer of water cascaded six or seven feet down the face of the rocks at a steady pace. A secret paradise, hidden deep in the woods and surrounded by thick foliage, a place very few people knew existed. I could see why the animals would come here to get a drink of water. I could also see how this could be a great place to hide something...

We made our way out of the brush and gathered in the small clearing that surrounded the pond. We were speechless at how beautiful and peaceful it was, hidden this close to the top of the mountain.

Chapter Nineteen

Lexi dipped her hand into the cool blue water and splashed some toward Buck. Startled, he jumped back and then quickly scurried back to retaliate, placing his hand in and splashing some toward her. The smiles raced across their faces. I grinned; it was nice to see Buck have a little fun.

"Enough," Parker yelled. "I thought we came here to look for a cave."

"You're right," said Buck, his face scrunched into a sly frown as he splashed water in Parker's direction.

Parker waved his hands in disgust and turned his attention toward the falls. I walked to the opposite side. Parker and I leaned forward in unison, reaching through the cold mountain water and placing our hands on the stone wall behind it. The rocks were smooth and covered in a thick slimy moss. We ran our fingers through it, over it, and under it trying to find an opening that the water might be hiding. Up and down the rocks we went, moving side to side, searching for an opening that might lead to the entrance of a cave. Several minutes passed resulting in nothing but cold fingers covered in nasty green slime.

"Nice smell," said Parker, taking a whiff of his fingers.

I followed suit, then curled my nose, and shook my head as a strong musty scent attacked my senses.

Scooter and Sara sat on some larger rocks next to the pond and watched the little stream of water trickle past, making its way down the slope.

"It makes you think, doesn't it?" Scooter asked, turning his attention to Sara.

"About what?" Sara asked, a surprised look on her face.

"About the water. It starts as a trickle and grows and grows into a larger stream and eventually makes its way to Fishing Creek. Have you ever wondered how long it takes for a single drop of water to reach the bottom of the valley and enter the creek?"

"Ah, no." Sara shrugged her shoulders. "I've never thought about it. It's almost like asking me if water has feelings like we do."

"I was thinking the same thing." Scooter seemed excited that they had the same thought.

"I think I'll help look for the entrance." She spun and began to look around.

Sara worked alongside Todd. They poked large branches into the nearby brush trying to reach the rock wall hidden behind. The foliage was dense. Who knew what lay beneath? They continued to poke and prod the bushes.

I heard the snapping of branches and noticed Todd bending and twisting them in all directions trying to get closer to the wall. He poked his stick at the rocks over and over again until he almost fell forward into the shrubbery when the stick hit an opening. "Hey, I got something!" he hollered to the rest of us.

Parker and Buck darted over to help with clearing a path to the wall. The wind rustled in the trees above us. A large gust of wind brought a chill with it. The clouds quickly rolled in and created a heavy, ominous feeling. The temperature felt like it had dropped ten degrees in a matter of seconds. The sky grew dark, and the wind whipped through the trees. Parker, Buck, and Todd continued to dig their way through the thick brush trying to reach the wall.

"There it is!" Parker said with excitement.

"We found it!" Buck hollered. "Nice job, guys!" Buck gave Todd a good hearty slap on the back.

"Thanks, dude," Todd replied, beaming with pride.

I felt giddy, like a child at Christmas. We had found it. I watched as the three of them cleared a large path to the entrance. Lexi, Sara, Scooter, and I closed ranks trying to look over their shoulders to catch a glimpse of the entrance. They handed us branches, and we cast them aside. In a matter of minutes, we had cleared enough brush to allow access to the entrance. *No wonder this cave had never been found.*

Jaggy, pointed edges of slate rock surrounded the three-foot by four-foot crack in the wall. "Hand me a flashlight," Parker belted out, holding his hand behind him, waiting for someone to put a flashlight in it. He continued to stare deep into the darkness. I quickly pulled a light from the backpack, flipped the switch on, and handed it to Buck, who passed the light to Parker.

Parker's hands shook as he directed the light into the cave. He poked his head in trying to get a better look.

"Are we going in?" Parker asked, looking back at the rest of us.

Scooter moved back to the large boulder some twenty feet away. Sara shrugged her shoulders and walked back to take a spot next to him with an unpleasant look on her face.

"I'm in," admitted Buck.

"Me, too," Todd added.

"Count me in," Lexi cheered

All eyes turned to me. "This is for Jimmy," I said with a wry smile on my face as I took a bold step forward.

Opening the backpack, I pulled out three flashlights and handed one to Buck and Todd, keeping one for myself. Lexi shook her head in agreement. I guess she planned on staying next to Buck. The five of us were all set to enter the cave. A large dark cloud hung overhead. The wind blew, and the temperature remained cold. I sure hoped it wasn't going to rain.

Parker glanced at his watch and turned to Scooter and Sara. "If we're not back in ten minutes, then... ah, who am I kidding? You won't come looking for us," he said as he entered.

"Not funny," Scooter barked. "If something happens, I'll go for help."

"Me, too," Sara called.

Serious for once, I turned to them and said, "If we're not back before dusk, please go for help." With that, I nodded my head once more and turned to enter the cave.

Scooter and Sara both agreed as they watched the rest of us duck down and squeeze our way into the cave. One by one, the flashlights flicked on and then vanished into the dark abyss.

A weird feeling settled over me. I wondered if Tom Evans or possibly even old man Smithers had followed us. Or what if they both had? At that moment, I was glad Sara and Scooter had stayed behind.

Chapter Twenty

A few feet into the cave, it opened up, allowing us to stand. The flashlight beams crisscrossed on the cavern walls. The temperature felt like a steady sixty degrees. The chill in the air made Lexi comment that she wished she had brought a sweater. From the looks of the cave, it went deep into the mountain. Parker took point, followed by me, then Todd, while Buck and Lexi decided to hang back and bring up the rear. She asked if any bats lived in the cave. I'm sure that's the last thing she wanted to see, but there was no way to know what we would find.

"You should be more worried about finding a bear instead of a bat," I teased.

I heard Buck whisper, "The entrance was too overgrown for a bear or any large animal to be living inside." He tried to reassure her.

One step at a time, the five of us slowly made our way deep into the cave—ten, twenty, now thirty feet deep in the cavern where I noticed many different rock formations. Small stalactites hung from the ceiling; underneath them were a few stalagmites that rose from the floor. I wondered how many years they had taken to form. I was glad I paid attention in science class.

The farther we went, the more the floor slanted downward. From the looks of things, we were descending deep into the mountain. We could see the ceiling was now about eight feet above us and about the same width from wall to wall.

We didn't hear a sound, just the cracking and grumbling of rocks under our shoes as we made our way down the long tunnel.

"What are we looking for?" Todd asked.

Parker turned to me. "This is your expedition, so what are we looking for?"

"I'm not a hundred percent sure, but I think we'll know when we find it," I said as we continued descending at a slow pace.

"Do you think there are any ghosts in here?" asked Lexi.

"I don't know," I honestly replied. "Considering the circumstances and what we witnessed last night in the attic, there might be. I mean, it's possible." My heart galloped a bit with the thought of coming face to face with a real ghost. I stopped and looked back toward the entrance, only to see a faint dim light cast from the outside.

* * *

I found out later that Scooter and Sara had talked about all sorts of odds and ends, nothing of any substance, just killing time. They were soon interrupted; the rustling of branches only twenty feet behind them had startled them.

"Is someone there?" Scooter asked, his voice a little shaky.

"Hello," Sara yelled, sounding a little more confident than Scooter.

The bushes moved again, along with a low growl. Scooter sat up straight, his eyes wide. Sara grabbed his arm and pulled herself closer to him. The two were terrified as they glanced left and then right. They were alone; none of the others was there to help. More moans and groans as the branches shook harder this time.

Two oversized crows flew in and settled on top the rocks that overlooked the waterfall. One of them squawked loudly. Scooter jumped, causing Sara to flinch as she turned around to look at the crows.

Sara pointed to the top of the ridge. "That's a really big crow."

"I've never seen one that size before," groaned Scooter. "Uhh, maybe we should have gone with the others?"

Bees buzzed around some of the flowery bushes, a dragonfly came in for a sip of water as he settled on the pond, and Scooter and Sara looked at each other trying to decide what to do.

* * *

Inside the cave, Parker mentioned we should turn off two of our lights to save batteries in case we needed them later. *Not a bad idea*, I thought. After all, none of us knew how old the batteries in the lights were or when they were even used last, not to mention we also didn't know how deep the cave went or how long we would be inside. It was harder to see with only two lights guiding the way, so we paused for a moment while our eyes adjusted to the darkness. The cave took a slight turn to the right and then back to the left. We no longer could see the light from the outside entrance.

"What's that?" I pointed.

"It's an old oil lantern," Parker said, reaching down to pick it up. "I wonder how old it is." We shook our heads, letting him know that none of us had any idea. Parker lightly waggled the lamp. "Nothing in it. That's a shame. We could have used the extra light." He snarled and placed the lamp back where we had found it.

We had taken only a few steps before the path turned to the right again. This time, the floor sloped downward about ten feet; it was also damp. Parker chuckled. "Anyone up for slip and slide?" He leaned back and laid a hand on the floor behind him, trying to avoid slipping as he gradually slid down the steep slope. We were probably about fifty yards into the cavern and possibly thirty feet deep, Parker shined his light on the slope so the rest of us could follow. Once we were all down the slope, we continued forward. The cave seemed to narrow again and turn once more to the left. Parker flashed his light from side to side and then backtracked the light, only to discover another opening in the wall.

"I think I found something." A little frightened, he paused before he poked his head around the corner and peered into an opening. We gathered behind him, trying to catch a glimpse; I stood on my tiptoes, straining to look over his shoulder.

"See anything?" Buck and Lexi asked at the same time. They giggled.

I stepped up beside Parker and flicked on my light. There was a small cavern alongside the main tunnel. The room looked to be narrow and stretched some twenty to thirty feet deep with a slight bend to the left.

"Can you see what's back there?" I asked, pointing to the left of the bend.

Parker shook his head as I turned to look at him. Laying a hand on the back of my shoulder, he shoved me forward through the opening. I stumbled a bit but quickly regained my balance.

"Go on, check it out," Parker said. "It's your baby. Now find your ghosts."

I was feeling a little pissed and nervous at the same time. *Why send the youngest in first? But he was right; this was my adventure.* I carefully placed one foot in front of the other, slowly making my way to the other side. Although the room was as cool as the rest of the cave, I could feel the sweat trickle down the back of my neck. I guess that was nerves. I shined the light in the direction of the corner. The room bent to the left side of the cavern where it opened up into a small pocket tucked away from the larger one. I ducked behind the small rock wall and disappeared. Ten, fifteen, twenty seconds had passed before Parker called out to me.

"You okay?" he asked. He shone his light around before calling out again. "Johnny?"

I smiled. It was time to get back at them. I remained silent. Looking around the small area, I could tell it was about six or seven feet in depth and nicely hidden behind the main wall. Just rocks and a slight trickle of water cascading down the far cave wall, nothing out of the ordinary.Then I paused when my light came upon a small wooden shovel leaning against the base of the wall. A few branches lay on the ground as well. *How odd, branches, yet no trees, and a shovel? What were they doing here?*

I heard Parker ask again if I was okay. An evil grin raced to my face when a plan flooded my brain. *It was payback time for all the times he and Buck had picked on me.* I screamed at the top of my lungs and waved the flashlight back and forth trying to imitate the signs of a struggle. Then I threw myself onto the ground. Only my legs were visible from behind the wall. I scurried forward using only my arms. "RUN!" I managed to scream as I turned my light off. Then I remained silent, covering my mouth so the others wouldn't hear my laugh. My screams echoed off the walls.

* * *

Buck told me later that Parker heard the scream and scuttled back. He shined his light back into the room only to see my legs pulled away and then vanish. "RUN!" He heard me shout and quickly jerked backward bumping into Todd then Buck and Lexi. The four of them started screaming and yelling as they broke and ran toward the entrance of the cave. Slipping and sliding up the steep incline and around the bend, they made their way back to the opening.

Outside, Scooter and Sara heard screaming. They quickly stood and darted toward the entrance. They hoped to catch a glimpse of what was happening. Then they noticed a light flashing over the walls and floor, quickly approaching. They spotted silhouette figures running in their direction. Frightened, they stepped back and waited for them to exit. One... two... three... four... they squeezed out of the entrance.

"Where's Johnny?" Scooter cried out.

"Something grabbed him...pulled him to the ground!" Parker exclaimed.

"What? And you left him there?" Scooter asked, stunned they left me behind.

"Not really," Parker said, shaking. "He's gone. You can't leave someone behind when they're gone."

"What do you mean 'gone'? We can't just leave him there," Scooter barked.

"He's right," Todd spoke up. "We have to go back and check."

Buck nodded in agreement, realizing what he had done. "My dad's going to kill me," he moaned. Lexi shook her head. She didn't appear to want to go back inside but knew that was the right thing to do. Parker remained silent, moving his hands around in front of him, not knowing what to do. "I just... I... I know what I saw; he's gone," Parker said and then bowed his head in shame.

Sara sat in silence, a tear tracing down her soft cheek.

* * *

"MISS ME?" I yelled, poking my head out of the crack in the wall.

Screams rang out as most of them leaped a few feet in the air. Scooter and Sara were the only ones who smiled. "You dork!" Todd yelled as he pushed me back against the wall. "You scared the crap out of us."

I laughed. "You should have seen your faces! You all acted like you'd seen a ghost."

"What the hell?" Parker yelled. "I saw them drag you away."

"That was sick, man," Buck said as he punched me in the arm. "But I'm glad you're okay." He smiled in relief.

Lexi paced around in disgust. "That was vicious, just downright uncalled for."

Sara sprang to her feet, happy to see me as she wiped the tears from her face. She ran to me, and engulfed me in the tightest hug I have ever received. I tried to step back, but she was not letting go.

"I'm sorry. I'm sorry," I repeated. "I was just having a little fun. I thought it would be funny. You know, payback for all the pranks you've played on me."

"It wasn't fun. It was downright wicked," Lexi grumbled as she continued to pace back and forth.

195

It didn't take long before everyone calmed down and saw the humor in my little prank. I heard Todd tell Buck and Parker, "You should have seen the look on your faces."

I blushed, trying to get Lexi to forgive me.

She was bitter, angry, and had every right to be. But in my defense, I was only getting back at her for the prank she played at the campsite that night.

Ten, maybe fifteen minutes passed before Lexi calmed down enough to listen. Buck placed his arm around her shoulder, trying to comfort her. It didn't take long before we were ready to venture back into the cave.

Twenty One

I explained what I found when I explored the smaller room. A very old shovel along with several branches from the trees. As Buck and Todd looked on, they didn't seem to be able to make the connection. Parker noticed it right away. "That's it," he whispered to himself.

"You say something?" Buck asked.

"That's it. It has to be it," he repeated a little louder.

"What's it?" Todd asked.

"Don't you see... the place where the old man buried the bodies? It has to be the spot," he said confidently.

I guess his statement drove it home as they murmured amongst themselves. Lexi perked up, saying she had been hoping to find the spot. Todd and Buck stood grinning from ear to ear. Parker's statement was beginning to sink in. I stood over by the entrance with a large smile on my face and nodded.

"What are we waiting for?" I blurted out, as I motioned for them to follow me back inside. I turned, squeezed through the opening, and started back down the long corridor, followed by Todd, Parker, Buck, and Lexi. Even Scooter and Sara were fascinated enough to follow us into the deep, dark cavern beneath the Earth's surface. *Would we solve the oldest murder in Lizardville?* My heart sang with the thought.

* * *

Little did we know that Mr. Evans lurked nearby, watching as we made our way into the cave. His chance had arrived. He pulled back the branches he was hiding behind, stood, and made his way to the entrance of the cave. He paused and then gradually stuck his head into the small opening. He noticed several flashlights dancing around in the darkness. He had no light of his own, so he decided to move quickly. Trying to use the light from the entrance and the light ahead as his guide, he stumbled on some loose gravel and fell and scraped the palms of his hands and knees. Scrambling to the side wall, he lay flat on his stomach on the cool, damp floor, trying not to reveal his location.

* * *

"Did you hear that?" I asked, my heart pounding as I came to an abrupt stop. The others quickly stopped, and everything fell silent. Looking around, Parker had shown his light forward and then backward. I did the same, even looking at the cavern ceiling to make sure there were no bats. "I swear I heard something," I said, then turned and proceeded deeper into the cave.

"What do you think we'll find?" Lexi asked Buck, her face beaming with excitement.

He smiled back at her. "A grotesque pile of flesh and bones, I would imagine."

Lexi balled her hand and punched Buck in the arm as the two smiled and flirted, giggling and laughing, trying to keep up with the rest of us. We approached the slick, steep slope, and one by one slid down toward the entrance of the hidden room.

I ducked my head as I entered the room. Parker followed along with the rest of us treasure hunters. We squeezed into the tight space, eagerly trying to catch a glimpse of what we might find.

Parker and I gradually made our way to the back corner of the cavern. Kneeling, I leaned forward and ran my hand over the top of the soil. Brushing the branches to the side, I paused, tilted my head, and glanced at Parker, who returned a slight smile and nod of approval. The dirt was solid. I tried to use my fingers to dig, but I made very little progress. I paused before I completely stopped; the dirt was just too hard. Parker reached forward, picked up the shovel, and pulled it toward him. He firmly gripped the handle and then shoved the flat end in the dirt.

* * *

Meanwhile, Mr. Evans had made his way deep into the cave. Stopping a few times to let his eyes adjust to the darkness, he heard our voices up ahead and spotted the soft glow of light coming from the entrance along the left wall. Quietly, he approached the flickering light that danced from the entrance. Our voices grew louder with every step he took. He paused and pressed his back against the wall, inching his way to the opening. Gently leaning forward, he poked his head around and spotted several of us gathered next to the base of the cavern wall. He watched as Parker and I worked on something hidden around the corner. He couldn't make out exactly what we were doing, so he decided to wait and listen.

* * *

Parker and I continued taking turns with the shovel. Sweat dripped from our foreheads. The process was slow and the ground hard. We tossed small loads of dirt to the side. The anticipation grew as the hole widened. We were making progress, a half shovel load at a time. Soon, we were pushing the two-foot mark. We paused to take a break. I turned my hands upward to look at the small blisters forming on my burning palms.

"How deep do you think we need to go?" Parker asked, his eyes fixed on mine.

"I don't know. I mean this has to be the spot… right?" I answered, doubt seeping into my voice.

We began to second guess ourselves. *This has to be the spot,* I thought to myself. *Why else would the shovel be here?*

Parker grabbed the shovel and plunged it back into the crater, removing a half shovel full of dirt. A few minutes passed; then a pungent aroma began to fill the cavern. A rotten stench was seeping from the ground. Parker and I were the first to smell it as it escaped the hole. I placed my hand over my mouth and nose. "Aaaaah, that's nasty," I scowled.

Parker backed up a little, making funny faces as he tried to ignore the smell. "That's worse than any fart I ever smelled!"

Buck, Lexi, and Todd stared at one another as if someone had farted. Sara and Scooter were the last two to smell the foul stench, strong and distasteful. They, too, covered their noses.

The soil had started to loosen. Parker picked up the shovel and thrust it back into the hole. It plunged deep into the ground, striking something soft. We both jumped back. Reaching up, he brushed the hair away from his face. We sat motionless, surprised. I reached in, grabbed the handle of the shovel, and pushed it downward again. This time what was underneath felt soft and spongy. I worked the shovel up and down then side to side, trying to clear a view of the object that lay just below the surface.

Parker reached in and used both hands to help move the earth. Tossing the shovel to the side, I did the same. The rubbery feeling soon turned out to be an old cloth of some sort. We pushed away the last mounds of dirt and opened the hole wider to uncover the remains of what looked like an old blanket. Steam omitted from the site, and the blanket began to crumble, exposing what lay beneath. What had been buried for over eighty years was now exposed to the elements. The fabric became brittle and slowly began to break. We ran our hands across the surface. The look on our faces said it all. We saw half of a human skull.

* * *

Joined by a smaller one, the two large crows sat patiently and waited above the cave's entrance. They quickly took flight, cawing as they rose high in the air. They circled above the cave opening, watching, listening, and waiting for the right moment.

* * *

Mr. Evans quietly listened from around the corner. He could tell we had uncovered something. Trying to get a better look, he was poking his head around the corner when Sara pointed one of the flashlights directly at him.

Spotting a pale white ghostly face gawking at us from the entrance, Sara screamed. Quickly, she pushed back against the wall and screamed again. Lexi looked toward the entrance, catching only a glimpse of something moving away. Hurriedly, we all moved back against the wall. The rocks' jagged edges poked our backs as we moved closer together. The figure disappeared and vanished out of site. Lexi screamed, "It's a ghost." Her voice quivered.

Parker and I pulled back and spun around trying to catch a glimpse, but the entrance was empty. We glanced at each other, shrugged our shoulders, and turned our attention back to the blanket that we slowly unearthed.

Mr. Evans must have been quietly nestled around the corner anticipating we would find him at any moment. Todd and Buck briefly looked at one another, turned, and tried to calm the girls, assurring them they could not have seen a ghost. Most likely, it was only their imaginations.

Lexi pointed to the entrance and whispered to Buck, "Please, make sure." She pouted a bit and watched Buck melt in front of her. I could see Sara's head bob agreeing with her sister.

I watched Buck, on hands and knees, doing as she commanded, slowly making his way to the entrance.

He glanced back at the girls, slightly smiling and trying to confirm he was right. He then poked his head around the corner and looked left and right. He seemed a little startled and jerked his head back inside. He took a few deep breaths and glanced around the corner again, this time tilting his head upward. A sigh of relief rushed through his veins. He smiled back at the girls then waved his hand, motioning for Todd to join him. Puzzled, Todd scuttled his way to the entrance. Buck pointed two fingers at his eyes, and then pointed around the corner.

Todd knew right away what he meant. He remained low to the ground and glanced around the corner. The two smiled as they stood up. Buck raised his right hand to coordinate the attack, slowly extending his fingers as he counted one, two, three.

As his third finger stretched out, he and Todd sprang around the corner, yelling and hollering, "Got ya! Got ya!"

Buck said Mr. Evans must have jumped six inches off the ground with both of his hands flailing around, acting like he was swatting flies.

Lexi and Sara both jumped back a little when they heard the boys struggling around the corner, but most of the sounds were coming from Mr. Evans.

Todd and Buck each grabbed an arm and pulled him to the opening for all of us to see. Startled and speechless, he began to calm down as did Buck and Todd.

Buck was the first to enter, followed by Mr. Evans, then Todd. Lexi dropped her chin with surprise. Sara was wide-eyed and shocked, and I wondered what he was doing here.

"Look who we got here," Buck announced. He and Todd stood straight, tall, and proud of their discovery.

Parker turned from our task; much to his surprise, it was Tom Evans.

I was the first to break the ice. "What are you doing here?" I blurted out, still toying with the edge of the blanket.

"I… I wanted," Mr. Evans fumbled with his words. "I was hoping you had, oh you know, opened the puzzle box and solved its clues. From the looks of it, you have," he sighed as if a great weight had been removed from his shoulders. "I'm sorry for following you. The story of the box has been passed down in my family for decades. I only wanted to know the truth. I knew you would solve it, Johnny; you're a smart boy. I know we've all had our differences in the past. If you let me stay, I promise that will change. Sometimes, I get this strange feeling that comes over me. Like someone or something has taken over my body, it's hard to explain."

I flashed back to that day in the store, remembering the dark look in Mr. Evans' eyes. The day of his accident, Jimmy must have had that feeling, too. That would explain a lot.

Parker was agitated and glared at Mr. Evans, forcing him to look the other way. We all could tell by the look on his face that he was ashamed. In a way, I could understand how he felt. But that still didn't give him the right to spy on us.

"I'm truly sorry. I am," he said. "Can I help in any way? Or, at least, watch, or offer support? After all, you wouldn't be here if it were not for the box."

He was right. I pondered the thought for a few seconds. Then I spoke, "I don't care if he stays."

"I don't either as long as you stay back there against the wall." Parker's response stunned us all. "This is our discovery," he warned.

Mr. Evans nodded in agreement, moving out of the way and leaning against the wall. He stood behind Buck and Lexi, looking into the hole and trying to catch a glimpse of what we had found.

I removed enough dirt to expose the edges of the brittle covering. Placing my hands at the corner, Parker and I worked together to fold the blanket back. A gasp of air escaped my mouth, and Parker's eyes widened at the sight of the skeleton.

A terrible squawking sound echoed off the walls. It quickly grew louder, the sound of wings flapping near the entrance made me turn my head. The temperature suddenly dropped ten maybe fifteen degrees, steam emitted from the exposed corpse, and the temperature continued to drop. Our heads turned to the opening as we tried to understand what was happening.

"STOP... STOP...STOP," a woman's eerie voice screamed.

Twenty Two

I quickly backed away from the grave and covered my ears, trying to drown out the loud shrill of the woman's voice as she continued to scream. I looked on and saw Mr. Evans and Lexi both doing the same as me. I watched them cower down, hands over the ears with their backs pressed firmly against the wall.

I turned toward the entrance, my face turning a pale white, paler than it already was. "Ah... oh, crap..." I cringed, stopping midsentence as a translucent figure stood blocking the entrance. The woman appeared to hover slightly off the floor.

Parker, Buck, Scooter, Todd, and Sara sat motionless in silence, puzzled at the scene unfolding before them. "What are they doing? What's going on? Why are they covering their ears and acting like that?" Parker questioned.

"Don't you see her? She's standing right there!" I screamed and pointed toward the entrance. "She's wearing a long white dress. And has dark bruising around her neck!" I trembled, yet still kept my ears tightly covered.

They shrugged their shoulders, unable to see or hear anything. I know they could see my breath in the air when I talked because I could see it. The temperature continued to drop in the room. The others began to feel the drastic change in temperature. I watched as panic set in on Sara and Todd.

The look on Mr. Evans' face was quite different, though. It was obvious that he could see what I saw.

"You had a daughter," Mr. Evans sputtered out. Then he paused, trying to gain his composure. "Her name was Elizabeth, right?"

"Don't you dare talk to me about my daughter!" the figure demanded, screaming back at him. She seemed furious about what we were doing in the cave.

I was shocked. She spoke, and I could hear her. From the look on Lexi's face, I could tell she heard her, too. I couldn't believe Tom Evans was talking to a ghost.

"Elizabeth," he spoke softly, repeating her name several times.

Annabelle's face softened on the words of her daughter's name as she stopped the shrill sound. "How do you know this?" she hissed.

"Your daughter Elizabeth grew up to be a lovely woman. She was in her mid-thirties when she met a nice man. They married and had a daughter. She named her after you. They called her Anna." He paused to take a deep breath and watched Annabelle's face sag. She seemed a bit puzzled. Tom continued, "Anna grew up and then later in life she married a man, a man named Tom, Tom Evans to be exact. Tom was my father, and Anna was my mother."

Annabelle gasped. "This can't be true. You lie!" she screamed at him.

"You're my great-great-grandmother," Mr. Evans' eyes teared up. His demeanor never wavered. "That's why I can see you. That's why you could possess my body. It all makes sense now." He smiled. "You look so much like the pictures I've seen of my grandmother, the ones my mother Anna showed me." He smiled reaching for his wallet and slowly pulling it out. He grabbed a picture and waved it in front of her face.

"Impossible," she said as a second ghost appeared standing next to her.

A tall, young man floated in alongside Annabelle. His shirt was tattered, torn, and sliced in many spots highlighted with dried dark red stains. He was still wearing the work clothes he had on the night Annabelle's husband killed him. He didn't say a word to anyone at first; he just gazed at the open grave. "I feel weak," he whispered to her.

"Cover the grave," she insisted. "Cover it now! Or you will all pay!" Her voice rose louder, her demands harsh as she made herself visible to everyone in the cave.

Sara and Parker heard a faint sound coming from the entrance, the silhouette of a woman floating in the doorway and another body standing next to her came into focus. Astounded and more frightened, they scooted back deeper in the cave and huddled in the corner. Tears ran down Sara's face, and it hurt me that I was unable to move to offer any comfort.

Scooter blinked several times trying to clear his eyes. Then he looked directly at the apparitions blocking the exit, unsure what to make of this new development. Buck and Todd were the last two who struggled to hear, see, or feel any of the changes that were taking place around us.

"One final warning, now cover the grave before you all pay!" she screamed, sending a rapid gush of wind through the small cavern with a stroke of her hand. She continued to swirl her hands around and around in a circle above her head, making the debris from the floor rise in a circular motion. Dirt from the floor floated in the air while Annabelle began to wreak havoc. Now she had everyone's attention, including the older boys. We all watched in disbelief when the small tornado whipped up in front of us.

"What… the… hell… is… going…on?" Buck managed to say, his voice quivering.

Todd raised his hands to cover his face. The dust stung as it spun around the room. "I don't like this, not one bit," he yelled, cowering in the corner. "My Aunt Carolyn in New Orleans is the one who believes in evil spirits, not me!" he shouted, trying to stay focused on the exit as another manifestation appeared. "I believe," he whimpered, lightly sobbing, "I believe, Aunt Carolyn. I believe."

Small pebbles and dirt continued to fly throughout the cavern, now at a much faster pace, along with a scattering of branches. We tried to take cover as best we could to avoid the flying debris. Annabelle demanded once again that we cover the grave, or none of us would make it out alive. "Stop," a familiar voice chimed in. "Please stop. These are my friends."

The smaller ghostly figure became visible, blurry at first and then more defined. Stepping forward, he spoke again. "You need to cover the grave. Do it now; do it quickly." Jimmy pointed to me. Annabelle stopped moving her arms, and the small tornado began to subside.

I sat on the floor, stunned and speechless, with Jimmy's ghostly figure standing before me, wearing no shirt, scruffy cut off jean shorts, and that old pair of sneakers, the same outfit he was wearing the day he died. My mouth agape, slowly, I regained my composure and did a double-take to make sure I wasn't dreaming. I came to my senses and crawled toward the open grave, keeping one eye glued to the exit. I took another glance at the three transparent figures—Annabelle, her lover, and Jimmy. I folded the blanket over the remains and gradually started pushing dirt over the grave. Parker wasted no time in scrambling to help.

Annabelle floated deeper into the room. You could see the reflection of burn marks around her neck. Relief cast over her face as her lover floated in beside her. Jimmy remained by the entrance, blocking our only exit.

I stood, unsure what to do next now that the grave was covered. Parker finished putting the last bit of dirt back over the hole and patted it down with his hands. I stepped forward and extended out my hand trying to touch Annabelle. She raised her hand toward mine, but our hands passed through each other. I shivered, the frozen air passing over my hand. "Don't you want to go home?" I asked gently.

"We are home," she replied with a wry smile. She glanced at the man at her side. "This is Jacob." Then turned back to Jimmy, who was making his way over to stand beside her and Jacob. "I think you know Jimmy." Her smile grew wider.

"I don't know what to say," I whispered and looked back at the others for words of wisdom. They remained crouched against the wall, nodding, slightly waving, and offering no advice at all.

"Jimmy, is that really you?" I asked in disbelief.

"It's me. I see you got the box open." He grinned.

"Ah, yeah, by accident and with help from Sara," I stammered, pointing in her direction.

She offered a little wave. Jimmy nodded back with a smile.

"Why?" I asked. "What about your parents? What about all of us?"

Jimmy smirked, but he didn't answer the questions. Annabelle laid her hand on Jimmy's shoulder and stepped forward. "I stepped into Jimmy's body that day on the creek, I wanted to learn his secrets, where he may have hidden the puzzle box, but time passes slowly on this side. Before I realized it, Jimmy had plunged over the falls. I was not able to help him after that."

We sat in silence as she continued. "People become ghosts when they're taken before their time. The same applies to me because I took my own life. We're forced to be here for all eternity to haunt the very place where we used to live. This is our curse to bear, but at least, we're all together," she spoke softly.

"If you pull Jacob's remains from the place where he rests, you'll send him to the other side, leaving myself and Jimmy alone forever, and I can't let that happen." She shook her head.

"If you ever come back here again," pausing, "I promise you, you will pay with your life."

Still in disbelief, no one moved. We took her threat seriously. Minutes passed, and, finally, Jimmy spoke again. "I'm happy here. I'm where I belong. It's a wonderful feeling. You should be happy for me." He smiled. "Now please, leave this place and never return."

We all smiled and nodded in agreement. This place would remain safe and hidden for a very long time if we covered the entrance back up.

Annabelle motioned it was time for us to leave.

Todd wasted no time, standing and darting toward the door, passing the ghosts, and avoiding any eye contact with them. Scooter went next, followed by Sara as they both scrambled by Jacob and Jimmy.

Lexi slowly stood and studied Annabelle for a moment. I think the two ladies shared some connection. "It was nice to meet you," she said as their hands passed through each other. Lexi grinned shyly. I noticed her body tremble a little before making her way out of the cavern.

Annabelle nodded in return, cracking a small grin.

Parker and Buck gradually moved toward the door. Jacob leaned forward to face them. "Boo," he said, and laughed as the two jumped back, pushing and shoving on one another, unable to get out of there as fast as they would have liked.

I frowned as I faced Annabelle. "I'm sorry. we didn't know."

"I don't want to lose him, and I know I can never leave this place." Sadness appeared in her eyes.

"Why wouldn't you be able to leave? Maybe we could help find a way." I offered.

"I took my own life, and this is my punishment, but I'm okay as long as I have my Jacob." She smiled and turned to face Jacob, admiring his smile.

I slowly walked toward the cave entrance. Stopping once, I turned and asked, "What about your husband?"

Annabelle sighed. "I haven't seen him in a few decades. I think he sleeps in a cave on the other side of the mountain. He was a lumberjack at one time, so he knows the woods well, better than the rest of us. You need to stay away from him. He's very bitter and angry. I think he would be very happy if Jacob crossed over. He enjoyed seeing me in pain."

Mr. Evans stood and faced Annabelle. He looked deep into her eyes. "I wish we could help," he said solemnly.

"You can. Stay away from here and stay away from that miserable old man I once called my husband. Oh, I almost forgot, there's one more thing…"

Tom perked up. "How can we help?"

"Bury the puzzle box with Jacob's body. We will keep it safe," she said with a smile.

"Give me one moment."

Mr. Evans came to the doorway where I stood. "Who has the puzzle box?"

I pointed to Buck, who had the backpack strapped to his back. He was standing about twenty feet away with Parker and Lexi at his side. "What is it?" I asked.

"We need to leave the puzzle box behind. I need to bury it with him. They can protect it," Tom explained.

I frowned and then turned to Buck. I held out my hand and asked for the backpack. Parker hesitated a few seconds, and I watched him and Buck squabble over what to do.

"Buck, Parker, this isn't your box; it's mine," I demanded. "Now give me the dang bag!"

Parker and Buck smirked at one another a bit in disbelief. Lexi whispered something to them, pressed her hand on each of their shoulders, and shoved them forward so they could hand the pack over to me.

I gladly took the backpack, opened it, and pulled out a small rolled up towel that contained the box. Slowly, I handed the towel over to Mr. Evans, who held it ever so gently as he gave me a half smile. "This is for Jimmy."

Ducking his head, he went back inside. I moved close to the entrance. I wanted to make sure he did what they ask. He picked up the shovel and carefully began to dig a small hole next to the grave. He carefully dug straight down, just a few feet I would guess. The hole looked just big enough for the box to fit. Annabelle, Jacob, and Jimmy circled him; they looked pleased when the box was laid to rest.

I watched Tom place the box into the hole and then cover it up as fast as he could. He and I looked at one another and said our final goodbyes to Annabelle and Jacob before making our way to the exit.

"Great-great-grandmother, will I ever see you again?" Tom asked.

"That depends on you." She paused and then cast him an odd look. "Let's hope not."

The three ghosts smiled and then faded when a gust of cold air whisked past us and out of the cave.

Wow, they were fast.

We walked toward the entrance of the cavern where the eight of us gathered around the small pond. Breathless, we gazed at one another. I think we were all still in shock. I couldn't believe what I just witnessed. Deep inside, I knew the truth: the legends were real. The ghost stories were true. There was no denying that now.

Buck and Parker sealed up the cave entrance as best they could by placing several larger rocks in front and adding extra brush to conceal it. They didn't want anyone else stumbling into this place by accident.

Sitting on top of the waterfall and observing our every move, sat two extraordinarily large crows and one smaller one. I think they were smiling down on us, watching, and knowing that they could trust us to keep their secret.

Our lives changed forever that summer. It was a summer I will never forget.

Twenty Three

Hours had passed since I started telling the boys my story. The wind still howled, rain pounded on the windows, and the storm raged on. The boys sat still, hinged on my every word. I think they were waiting for more. I smiled, my eyes fixed on Daniel before turning to Zack. I waited for comments or questions.

A few more moments passed before Zack finally spoke. "WOW! What a story! Is any of that true?" he asked squirming a little, with both hands tightly gripping the arms on the chair.

I smiled. "Of course, it's true, every last word of it."

"Dad, did you really see three ghosts when you were a kid?" Daniel asked.

I slightly nodded. "Yes, I did."

"Did you ever see any of them after that day?" asked Zack.

"Well, in fact, we did. We saw the crows several times and even spent more time with Jimmy and Annabelle, but that's a whole other story, one that I'll save for another day," I said when I spotted head lights rolling into the driveway. "I think your mother's home," I announced to the boys.

Smiling, they jumped up, ran to the door, and waited for her. Another crack of thunder was accompanied by a bright flash of light that came shooting across the room as Mother opened the door. The boys jumped back as she stepped in and lay her umbrella to the side.

"Hi, boys." She grinned, wrapping her arms around them in a giant size hug. "I can't stay long. They need me back at the hospital. I just came home to get something to eat and check on you three," she said. Then she noticed a strange look in the boys' eyes. She walked over and gave me a kiss on his cheek. "You haven't been telling ghosts stories, have you?"

I looked away, shrugged my shoulders slightly, and then shook my head. "What do you mean?" My glimpse over her shoulder toward the boys gave me away. She turned to face the boys, who stood in silence, like two boys who'd been caught telling a lie.

"Has your father been telling you ghost stories?" she demanded.

Their eyes widened, and a funny look shot across their faces. I knew I was busted. Sara had everything she needed to know the truth. "Oh, John, I hope it wasn't the Lizardville stories." She paused. "John, you know these boys won't sleep for a week; those stories will scare the crap out of them." Facing me, she gave me a stern look.

"Sorry," was all I could muster along with a frown.

"Mom, did you and Dad see a ghost?" Zack asked.

"Well," she said, leaning forward and placing her hands on her knees. She drew in as close as she could and looked directly into each of their eyes. She never faltered as she whispered these words, "Let me ask you one question…" The boys grew excited as they waited for her response. "Do you believe in ghosts?" She raised her eyebrows as her wide eyes bounced back and forth between the two.

Saying nothing else, she turned toward me, winked, and strode toward the kitchen with a smile.

Acknowledgments

To my loving wife Toni, Thank you for all your support and help while I was writing this story.

Thank you to my four wonderful daughters, Kim, Kelly, Jessica, and Ashley for all your support and encouragement.

Thank you to my parents Charlie and Joanne for believing in me and buying a home in Lizardville.

Thanks also to all the beta readers, Melissa Derr, Silvia Curry, Carolyn Hornick, Irene Blitch, Connie Headrick, Jim Dodds and Toni Altier for your sharp eye and helpful hints.

Special thanks to Adele Brinkley with Pen In Hand Editing service; I couldn't have done this without you.

Learn more about Steve Altier and his stories by following on Facebook or visit his website.

www.stevealtier.com

https://www.facebook.com/SteveAltierauthor

Sign up for quarterly news letters or just say hello to Steve via email at: **stevealtierbooks@outlook.com**

Author Bio

Steve Altier was born in a small town in central Pennsylvania. Aka "Lizardville" He currently lives in the Tampa Bay Metro area with his wife. Steve has four daughters and three loving cats.

He enjoys writing, reading, bowling, and spending time at amusement parks. He loves to travel, take trips to the beach, or just laying around the pool spending time with family and friends. With his vivid imagination, he enjoys writing YA and MG children's stories.